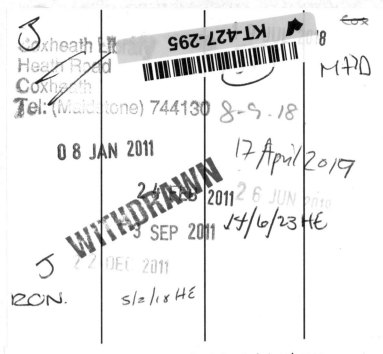

DELUGE!

When Jeff Alroyd rides into a divided valley, he discovers that the Circle C Ranch, owned by Babs Kemp and her father, is under threat because adjoining landowner 'Poker' Barrow has sabotaged their stream. Jeff Alroyd is determined to help Babs by using his expertise as a mining engineer and poker player. Jeff outwits Barrow and regains the stolen water, but when Barrow resorts to murder and kidnapping, Jeff finds himself apparently beaten — without money, pipeline or water.

ARNOLD RYDEN

---◆---

DELUGE!

Complete and Unabridged

LINFORD
Leicester

First published in Great Britain in 2000

Originally published in paperback as
Gunsmoke Valley by John Russell Fearn

First Linford Edition
published 2010

British Library CIP Data

Ryden, Arnold.
  Deluge!. - - (Linford western library)
  1. Western stories.
  2. Large type books.
  I. Title II. Series III. Fearn, John Russell,
  1908 – 1960. Gunsmoke valley.
  823.9′14–dc22

  ISBN 978–1–44480–167–5

Published by
F. A. Thorpe (Publishing)
Anstey, Leicestershire

Set by Words & Graphics Ltd.
Anstey, Leicestershire
Printed and bound in Great Britain by
T. J. International Ltd., Padstow, Cornwall

1

Jeff Alroyd came through Demon's Head Pass towards sunset. It was at the hour when the western sky of Texas was painted in Nature's most flamboyant colours, the crags and domes of the Apache Mountains looming black against a tracery of salmon-pinks and incredible greens. Seasoned as he was to such lavish displays of Mother Nature's brush, Jeff Alroyd did not take any particular notice. The sky, peaceful or tempestuous, was something which he had always taken for granted. Its changing moods were for the stranger, not for the hard-bitten man of the Western plains . . .

Presently he drew his mare to a halt, leaned on the saddle horn and looked pensively about him.

He was tired: he had travelled a long way through the burning heat of the desert. Even his mount was nearly too weary to carry him — but she gathered some strength as the sound of cascading water fell upon her sharp ears. She turned and loped along with head down, following the rough pathway, nor did the man in the saddle try and stop her.

When at length she came to a broad, fast moving stream springing from somewhere underground the man dropped from the saddle and bathed his face and hands in the cool water following it up with a long, deep drink. Refreshed again he stood looking about him as the mare drank her fill.

On two sides were the mountains — invincible, climbing in crag, buttress and peak to the amazing sky. Behind was the trail which led from the desert, and in front — The traveller cuffed up his dusty black Stetson on to his forehead and gave a slow grin. Ahead was a valley, and roughly in the centre of it lay a ranch and a big corral. The ranch-house windows were gleaming in the light of oil lamps. They seemed like a welcome after the long journey he had made.

'I reckon we might be able to bed down for th' night there, Smoky,' he murmured to the mare, patting her broad nose as she straightened up from the stream. 'The folks at the ranch might well start raisin' objections to havin' a footloose stranger like me in their midst — but leastways we can try. Pretty well the law of the West that one should be a good neighbour, 'specially a couple as dusty as we are . . . Let's be movin', shall we?'

He vaulted back into the saddle and turned the mare's head round. At a jog-trot Jeff Alroyd began to follow what he had at first taken to be the trail's continuation, but the further he went the more it became clear to him that he was in the midst of what had once been a watercourse — and not so very long ago, either. Even the smooth, flat-headed stones which had lain under the fast moving water had not yet become covered with a deep layer of prairie and mountain dust. No; this was no ancient arroyo, but one which had only recently come into being. It was the kind of phenomenon he had not often seen — and it puzzled him.

'Looks like there's some kind of a change in the landscape around here, Smoky,' he murmured in the mare's ear as they progressed. 'Mebby that stream we stopped at got diverted by some kind of natural phenomenon. Does happen sometimes, 'specially in the mountains . . . But if it comes to that what in the heck am I worrying about?'

Since the matter was of no particular interest to him he forgot all about it as he continued his leisurely way into the valley — but it was forced back into his mind as, presently, he began the journey across the valley floor to the ranch he had selected as a possible sanctuary for the night.

Even now the light had not all gone from the western sky: it was still strong enough for him to see a vast, arid, wilting area, blistered by the merciless Arizonian sun, powdered with fine dust, in the midst of which the grass was withered and chippy.

This appalling dryness extended as far as he could see ahead of him — but halfway down the valley, on his right, the bareness appeared to shade off into a deep, lush green which bespoke a plentiful water supply. Down here in this valley two conditions lay uneasily side by side. There was death, where he now moved, and — two miles away — life rampant and full of promise. It was to him a most curious sight. He was accustomed to the magnificent pastures of the well watered areas, or the utter deadness of the desert — but for the two to be present within a few miles of each other was definitely unusual. It set him thinking again about the newly created arroyo he had just traversed. 'It's queer, Smoky — durned queer,' he muttered. 'Sort of reminds you of the fat and lean years, I reckon . . .'

As if to confirm his conviction that he was riding through a death area he saw on approaching the solitary ranch that the corralled cattle were thin. Some of them had their bones riding visibly against their hides. There was a lowing and shifting in the dusty, gathering night — the moaning of beasts ill-fed and profoundly uneasy.

Jeff Alroyd rode across the yard to the ranch-house porch and then dropped from the saddle, tying his mare to the porch rail. He strode up the three steps and knocked on the screen-door. From the look of the place, its obvious atmosphere of disuse and the forlorn appearance of the cattle, he expected to meet a hard-faced degenerate who had gone to the bad through drink, or else somebody who was too old to handle things properly any more.

His surprise was therefore absolute when a girl opened the screen-door and looked out upon him in the dying light.

'I — er — ' Jeff tugged off his stetson quickly. ''Evenin', ma'm,' he said awkwardly.

The girl did not respond to his greeting. He could not see her very clearly but what few details were apparent revealed a youthful, well-moulded figure and a tumbled mass of fair hair. A check shirt and blue levis tucked into high-heeled half-boots did nothing to detract from her lithe grace. He fancied he caught a faint gleam in her eyes as at length she stirred.

'Good evening,' she responded, and evidently she too had been engaged in summing up. 'Is there anything I can do for you, stranger?'

She had a soft, cultivated voice which bespoke education. 'Well, yeah — I reckon there is,' Jeff assented. 'Y'see, I'm — I'm lookin' for a spot to bed down for the night. I c'n pay,' he added hastily.

'Why should I doubt the fact?' the girl said quietly.

'Well, only because I'm lookin' pretty dusty an' unshaven but I'm no saddle tramp. I've come clear across the desert and this happened to be the first ranch

7

I set eyes on. It started getting dark, so I figgered . . . '

'You'd better come in and see my father,' the girl said, pulling the door wide open. 'This is hardly the kind of business I can arrange myself. Come along . . . '

'Thanks, ma'm. It's mighty decent of you.'

Hat in hand Jeff strode with long legs into the ranch-house living room. It was long-walled in the conventional style, weather proofed with red clay. The furniture was sufficient, but rustic. A skin rug lay before the newly-made and crackling fire. There was a homeliness, a cheering warmth, about the place.

At the table, apparently going through a pile of correspondence, was a silver-haired man with stern eagle-like features. His deep blue eyes glanced up and then studied Jeff in the glow from the lamps.

'Howdy,' Jeff greeted quietly. 'Sorry to barge in, but I — That is, the young lady here . . . '

'A stranger, Dad,' the girl explained,

coming foward. 'He says he's looking for somewhere to spend the night. So I said he'd better see you. From the looks of him he's been riding the trail pretty hard, and his mare is nearly fagged out too.'

The silver-haired man rose to a full six-feet-three. He was unusually massive, but past the prime of life. The tan of his features, a deep burned-in brown, bespoke the man who had lived his life the hard way in the western open spaces. He had a simple honesty in his expression which instantly won Jeff's confidence.

'Glad to know you,' he said, and held out his gigantic hand. 'We don't get many strangers around these parts — an' even when we do I don't always make 'em welcome.' There followed a long, relentless scrutiny from the blue eyes; then, 'I reckon I know the ones I can trust. But you won't mind me askin' you where yore from?'

'Kansas — originally. I've been moving around in hops . . .' Jeff gave his infectious grin. 'I'm a mining engineer — or was. Jeff Alroyd's the name.'

'Alroyd?' The old man frowned. 'Mmmm — seems like I heard that name somewheres . . . Anyway, I don't s'pose it matters. So yore just sort of wanderin'?'

'You might call it that. I've inherited a footloose streak and it makes me wander off before I can start to settle down. When the yen comes I just quit whatever I'm doing and hit the trail . . . This time I'm heading no place in partic'lar. If you can bed me down and let me stable my mare I'll be on my way again at sun-up.' Jeff paused and then added quietly, 'I can pay for it, and I'd be mighty glad if . . . '

'Keep your money son,' the old man interrupted. 'I haven't gotten to the place yet where I ask a traveller to pay for stayin' the night under my roof — an' I hope I never shall. Yore more 'n welcome.'

Again the scrutiny. Jeff accepted it without flinching. The old man's fierce gaze went over a tall, rangy figure, muscle-packed, brown-faced, black haired, with faintly humorous grey eyes and a broad mouth and chin. The gaze dropped to twin .45s packed in their holsters, and to a pair of hands which were obviously not unacquainted with hard work.

'I'm Morton Kemp,' the old man said, the scrutiny finished. 'This is my daughter Barbara — or Babs, as I call her. She's had an education back east. I've had none, but I'm not ashamed of it. Isn't so important fur a man to be educated as it is for a gal. Babs came back to help me with the spread when her mother died a couple years back. The way things have gone, it's mebby just as well she did die,' the old man mused, rather ambiguously.

Jeff said nothing because he was feeling unaccountably embarrassed.

'My father takes things the hard way sometimes,' the girl hastened to explain — at which her father turned and looked at her.

'Yeah, mebby I do at that,' he

admitted. 'But when you git to my age you git to thinkin' on the things that have happened an' what some folks have missed. Then you . . . ' Kemp dropped the subject — if subject it could be called — as suddenly as he had brought it up.

Jeff's eyes strayed from the towering old rancher to the girl. Now he could see her clearly his first impression that she was highly delectable was confirmed. She was not quite a beauty, but she was certainly pretty. In her case the deep blue eyes of her father had become violet, and there was definitely no bleach to account for the wealth of corn-coloured hair. Her nose was straight, her mouth small and upturned at the corners. As for her chin, it was rounded and firm and said that she knew her own mind.

'Babs'll show you where you c'n stable your horse and then freshen yourself up,' Morton Kemp said abruptly. 'We'll be havin' supper then. It must be 'bout time.'

'I'm mighty obliged to you, Mr Kemp . . .'

'Think nothin' of it, son.' The old man jerked his head to the girl. 'Fix him up, Babs, while I clear away these all-fired papers . . .'

The hospitality of the big, silver-haired rancher and his daughter went beyond anything Jeff had expected. He had hoped for the ready hand of a good neighbour, but he had certainly never expected such open cordiality. The girl and her father fed him and talked to him like an old friend as the meal progressed, so much so that he could not help but feel it would be in order if he posed one or two questions.

'I don't rightly know how you'll take this,' he said, looking first at the girl then at her father, 'but it seemed to me when I rode up to this spread tonight that I smelled death.'

Neither the girl nor her father spoke. They just sat waiting, expressionless.

'And I smelled it in the valley too,' Jeff added. 'It's a bone dry wilderness just around here, though I don't suppose you need me to tell you.'

Morton Kemp gave a slow grim smile.

'No, I reckon we don't,' he agreed, shaking his head. 'You wouldn't think it, but a year ago this ranch — the Double Circle as it's called — was one of the most thriving hereabouts. Now it's dyin' — an' fast — and there's just plain nothing we can do about it.'

'And yet you stay on here?' Jeff asked, puzzled. 'I think that if I had found things around me had gotten into such a mess I'd be on my way mighty quick. Seems kind of silly to stop, doesn't it?'

'I s'pose it does, to a stranger.' The old rancher spoke thoughtfully, sitting back in his chair. 'But y'see son, Babs and me have sort of gotten the idea that since an accident deprived us of our livin' another accident might bring it back — in the twinkling of an eye, as y'might say.'

Jeff only looked all the more bewildered, then he turned to the girl as she began to explain.

'Up to a year ago, Mr Alroyd, this ranch was one of the most prosperous in Double Peak Valley. At that time we had over two hundred head of cattle, and all of them thriving. Trade was brisk with the cattle dealers: we had pasture second to none hereabouts. Then — overnight — it all vanished . . . ' The girl's pretty face assumed a desolate expression for a moment. She went on talking with something of an effort:

'There was an avalanche in the Apache Range and the rocks blocked the stream which irrigated our pastures. The water turned north and nourished the opposite end of the valley. Whilst our land died, 'Poker' Barrow's blossomed out, and changed him from a very ornery rancher into a wealthy cattleman. That's the reason for the arid land and rich pasture lying side by side — and we've gotten the worst of it.'

'Yeah, I can see that,' Jeff mused. 'And you've my sympathy, too . . . An' who's 'Poker' Barrow, anyway?'

The girl laughed slightly. 'His real name's Vincent Barrow, but since he's always playing poker in his spare time — and nearly always winning — he's acquired that nickname. He's our nearest neighbour, about three miles from here. I see quite a good deal of him.'

'Durned sight too much, if you ask me,' the old man growled. 'I don't like the critter, and never did. He wasn't so bad while he hadn't made himself much of a ranch, but since water transformed his spread he's become too big for his hat. I reckon I never saw such a change in a feller. Looks like he was only holdin' himself down until somethin' came along to boost him up.'

Though Jeff knew he had no possible right to feel jealous, he did just the same. In fact he was quite convinced that he hated 'Poker' Barrow more than anybody else in the world. In the very short time he had come to know Babs Kemp she had become extraordinarily important to his scheme of things.

'Gambling was the only thing which kept Poker alive during the lean years,' the girl said, thinking.

'Look here . . . ' Jeff shifted his position and frowned. 'Look, if he's got your water, isn't there somethin' you can do about it? What's the law for? Your spread just can't be allowed to fold up and die, surely?'

'There's nothin' we can do,' Morton Kemp said, his tone completely final. 'I've bin into it all, as you may be sure — but in these parts you've either got water or you ain't. That change in the course of th' stream is legally classed as an 'Act of God'. It killed our spread and brought Barrow's spread to life — Just his luck and our misfortune. Ain't nothin' nobody can do about that, I reckon.'

'We did try and make a deal with him,' the girl added. 'A sort of half and half arrangement, but there was nothing that could be done. Not even blasting could clear the rocks so half of the water could come our way.'

'So,' Jeff asked, 'you just sit here in the cemetery and wait for a happy accident to change your fortunes?'

'Sounds loco, mebby, but it's all we can do,' Morton Kemp responded, hunching one shoulder, ''less somebody comes along an' buys the spread for what it's worth. It's in the market an' has bin for some months. If that happened, Babs and me could get out to a fresh place or somethin'. At my age, though, I'm none too keen on startin' again. I'm sixty-five, an' it takes youth — like Babs here with her twenty-five years — to do things.'

The girl coloured slightly at her father's bland revelation of her age, and Jeff gave a faint smile.

'Even the boys have left us,' Babs hurried on, changing the subject. 'Our foreman's gone, and the punchers just drifted away one by one. What there is to do we do ourselves. But it's the awful feeling of sliding downhill which — '

She broke off at a sudden emphatic

banging on the outside of the screen-door. Hurriedly she got to her feet and moved across to the mirror over the mantle. Tidying her hair with a few swift judicious pats she said quickly:

'I expect that'll be Poker. He said he'd be coming over this evening.'

Her father sniffed with profound contempt.

'If there's one thing I wish in this world,' he muttered, as the girl left the room. 'It's that she wasn't so keen on that guy Poker. She's a headstrong gal, though, so there ain't so much I c'n do about it.'

'No, I reckon not,' Jeff agreed, and could not think of anything further to say. He moved position slightly and sat waiting interestedly for a glimpse of the man whom he knew he was going to dislike more than anybody else in the world. Nor did he have to wait long.

The man who came in behind the girl was a six-footer, handsome after a fashion, and still in the early thirties. He evidently took himself seriously for he was attired after the fashion of a prosperous rancher with a big expanse of white shirt front down which dangled a shoe-string tie. Twin guns appeared transiently at his thighs as his jacket moved back in his advance across the room.

'Company, huh?' He glanced at Jeff in surprise.

'Just passin' through,' Morton Kemp explained. 'Jeff Alroyd — Vince Barrow.'

Jeff rose, shook hands, and nodded. The dark, luminous eyes of Barrow looked him over with a certain contempt. It made the short hairs bristle on the back of Jeff's neck.

'Passin' through, eh?' Barrow repeated. 'Well, I reckon that's all right then.'

'Is it?' Jeff gave a faint smile. 'Don't take it as dead certain. I might change my mind and stick around. It depends how much I like the district. When I get a likin' for a place I've a habit of stickin' — sometimes for years.'

'If you like this district — an' this spread — yore plain crazy,' Barrow told him frankly. 'It's dyin' faster than a sunset — or was it too dark for you to notice as you came in?'

'I noticed,' Jeff replied, and sat down again languidly. 'But I'm still not sayin' I dislike the district.'

The girl looked from one man to the other somewhat uneasily, then she turned her attention to Barrow as he strode over to her.

'What's the idea?' he asked, and his hand flicked contemptuously at her check shirt. 'I didn't come here to take a cowgirl out for the evenin'. I thought you'd be dolled up ready for our night out.'

'Yes, I know — I did promise, didn't I?' Babs gave a hurried smile. 'Matter of fact I forgot we'd arranged to go into town for the evening. So many things have been happening. Then there was Mr Alroyd — '

'There was, eh?' Barrow interrupted her and glanced at Jeff coldly. 'What's he got to do with it? Did I make an appointment or didn't I?'

'Yes, of course you did — but I had to fix up Mr Alroyd, and it all took time.'

'If you ask me, Babs, this big stranger looks as though he's well capable of fixing himself up. Don't need a gal to run about after him, surely?'

'There's such a thing as hospitality,' the girl retorted, an edge in her voice.

'Okay, okay!' Barrow raised his big hands placatingly. 'You'd better start gettin' ready an' be quick about it.' He threw himself in an armchair and added, 'I don't like bein' kept waitin'.'

The girl hesitated and then turned and left the room, shutting an adjoining door. Barrow passed a lean, long-fingered hand over his dark hair. His eyes slanted towards Jeff in sudden suspicion.

'I reckon you must have made quite an impression on Babs for her to forget her date with me, stranger,' he commented. 'Congratulations.'

Jeff said nothing. He went on eating, undisturbed.

'I dunno what the gal wants to go out

at all for!' her father objected. 'How'll you spend the evenin', anyway? I'll tell you! You'll just yank her to the Twin Dollar and then start gamblin' whilst she has t'sit an' wait. That ain't no life for a gal who's been decently educated.'

'Education doesn't count for much in these parts, pop,' Barrow assured him. 'Besides, there's nothing else to do around here. Babs might as well get used to it. Have to break her in for when we get married, don't I?'

Jeff chewed a piece of bread steadily as he met the cold grin of Barrow across the table.

'Cattle man, stranger?' Barrow enquired suddenly.

'Nope.'

'Just a saddle tramp, then?'

'Nope . . . ' Jeff took a long drink from his coffee cup.

'In fact you don't intend to say what you are?' Barrow asked grimly.

'Can you think of any good reason why I should? You're not the sheriff, are you?'

Poker scowled slightly. 'Okay, feller, but don't start getting any fancy ideas, that's all. I'm warning you I'm the biggest man around these parts and I got here first.'

'Sure you did,' Jeff agreed. 'Has to be an end to everythin', though, I reckon.'

'If yore aimin' to make trouble, stranger, you'd best not!' Poker snapped, his tan deepening. 'I know just what you're thinkin' — that Babs Kemp is a mighty pretty gal. Not that I blame you. You wouldn't be human if you didn't think that — but don't let it go any further.'

Jeff only smiled and put down his coffee cup, then his eyes lifted as the girl reappeared from the bedroom. Her cowgirl attire had vanished and given place to a flowered frock which revealed the still girlish curves of her figure to perfection. Slight make-up — evidently a practice she had cultivated when away for her 'education' — enhanced the prettiness of her features and lent a depth to her violet eyes.

'Pretty as a picture,' Barrow commented,

getting up and kissing her with unnecessary emphasis. 'Okay, let's go. I've got my buckboard waitin'.'

The girl nodded and took down a dustcoat from behind the door.

'Oh, just to show you how generous I am,' Barrow added, pausing and glancing back at Kemp. 'I've decided I might as well buy this spread of yours. You've had it up for sale long enough and I've refused. Now I've thought better of it . . . Only fair that I should, I s'pose, seein' as yore the father of the girl I'm aimin' to marry.'

Alertness came to old man Kemp. 'What figure are you aimin' to pay, Poker?'

'Two thousand dollars — Yeah, I know it isn't much, that it's fifteen hundred below what yore askin' — but look what sort of a ruin it is! No water, cattle dyin', and yore never likely to get anybody else comin' this way who'll pay the price you want. You'd best think it over, pop. When I bring Babs back later I'll be expectin' an answer.'

'You can have it right now,' Jeff said. 'Mr Kemp isn't selling.'

There was complete silence. Morton Kemp stared fixedly at Jeff and then frowned hard. The girl half opened her mouth to say something, and then refrained. Barrow lowered his arm from about her slim shoulders and came forward to the table. He stood leaning forward with his knuckles pressed hard into it.

'What was that you said?' he demanded.

'Your ears full of mountain dust?' Jeff enquired. 'I said there's no sale, and I'm not the kind of guy who likes to have to keep repeatin' things. I guess you heard me all right.'

''Course I heard you, but what I want to know is who in the blue thunder are you to answer, anyways?'

'I'm a mining engineer.' Jeff gave a slow, taut grin. 'You asked me a while back what I am. Now you know. If you have as much brains as you have swank you'll probably guess what I'm driving at, or maybe the fact that I'm a mining engineer doesn't mean anything to you?'

'A mining engineer, eh?' Barrow's dark eyes narrowed. 'An' because of you being that you reckon you can see possibilities in this spread? Even as it stands?'

'Yeah — and those possibilities are worth a darned sight more'n two thousand greenbacks.' Jeff got to his feet and ambled round the table, his thumbs hooked in his gunbelts. He stopped in front of Barrow and eyed him thoughtfully. 'Somehow,' he said, musing, 'I've taken a plain dislike to you, feller. Kind of thing I do sometimes. You're a bit too free with your tongue — and your mitts.'

Barrow swallowed hard and glared. 'You've some damned cause to talk! You come breezin' in from no place and start sayin' what you think about me! If you figger I'm the kind of guy who'll stand for that kind of thing yore crazy!'

'Okay, I'm crazy,' Jeff said simply;

then he glanced across at the girl as she stood waiting beside the outer door. 'You going with this guy because you want to, Miss Kemp, or because it's a habit?' he asked.

'Well, I — After all, I had sort of arranged . . . ' The girl stopped, in obvious confusion.

'Then I reckon you'd better give it some proper reflection,' Jeff commented. 'I don't somehow like the thought of this jigger kissin' an' maulin' you around. You don't look like that kind of girl to me — ' He swung abruptly on the glowering Barrow. 'You can find plenty of wornouts in the Twin Dollar who'll do what you want in return for a drink,' he snapped.

Barrow's rage spilled over. His hands blurred down to his guns, but never reached them. Casually Jeff kicked out his toe — hard. It cracked across Barrow's shin and made him gasp. He doubled, then straightened, as a terrific backhander under the chin sent him flying backwards across the room.

Dazed, he brought up with a crash against the fireplace.

'Get out,' Jeff ordered quietly, one of his own .45s levelled. 'I don't like snakes.'

Barrow straightened up, fingering his jaw. Finally he picked up his fallen hat, seemed about to say something, and then thought better of it. He left with quick, angry strides and slammed the screen-door behind him. An astonished silence remained behind which was broken at last by a chuckle from old man Kemp.

'I'll be dad-blamed if I ever saw anythin' like it!' he exclaimed. 'I just knew I had you figured right, Jeff, when I first set eyes on you — Now I'm convinced of it. I've bin wantin' to send that guy packin' for long enough, but somehow I always felt that I mightn't be fast enough. He's a darned sight younger than I am, an' if it came to drawin' — '

'Do you realise what you've done, Mr Alroyd?' the girl broke in anxiously, coming forward with wide eyes. 'Poker's one of the most powerful men in Double Peak. He'll start gunning for you after this. I never knew him to let up on a man once he's taken a dislike to him.'

Jeff holstered his .45. 'Okay. Let him start gunnin'.'

'But you don't understand — '

'Listen, Miss Kemp.' Jeff took her arm gently to add emphasis to his words. 'Because this part of the world isn't particularly careful about its laws some jiggers make it an excuse to manhandle women. I've bin around plenty and I've seen so much of it it made me sick. That's never been my code. To me a woman's always a woman, and I'll protect her if need be — pretty or ugly, old or young. That's all I did tonight — an' if 'Poker' Barrow tries anythin' on me he'll soon find out that I didn't learn to start shootin' yesterday.'

Babs drew away from him, gazing in amazement.

'I — I don't think I ever met a man quite like you before,' she breathed. 'Not in these parts . . .'

'If Barrow is your best experience, you sure didn't,' Jeff agreed, grinning.

'He'll do just anything now,' she insisted. 'You've come between him and me and — '

'The point is, do you love him, or even want him? That's what I want to be knowing.'

'No — not any more. In fact I doubt if I ever did.' The girl drew the back of her hand over her lips and winced. 'He never behaved before as he did tonight. That kiss of his positively hurt!'

'It was meant to,' Jeff said grimly. 'In fact I'll wager he did it just for my benefit. Anyway, he got revealed in his true colours, which is one good thing, and to my mind getting booted off the premises is the very least he deserves.'

'I don't rightly see,' old Kemp said, standing up, 'why you turned down that offer of his for this spread. Was it to spite him, to stop him having any connection with Babs, or what?'

'It was to save you from being gypped,' Jeff answered. 'When I heard him make that offer I got to thinkin' as to why it had been made. It didn't make sense for a place which is obviously dyin'. Then it dawned on me what the game was — an' so I decided to stop him. There wasn't time to ask you about it so I just acted — an' decided to take my chance on explaining things afterwards.'

'But this place is dead,' the girl declared, tossing down her dustcoat. 'It's absolutely sucked dry by the sun!'

'It can be watered again,' Jeff said, with quiet assurance. 'I'll show you just how tomorrow mornin' . . . Which means,' he added, 'that I shan't be aimin' to hit the trail again just yet.'

'You'd better not!' old man Kemp exclaimed. 'More I see of you, son, the more I think yore the kind of feller this ranch has been needin' for some time.'

Jeff sat down again at the table and

his eyes travelled over the girl as she looked at him pensively.

'Just what I was thinking,' he murmured. 'Now, how's about some more coffee?'

2

If 'Poker' Barrow had any schemes in mind for retaliating they certainly did not mature during the night. Jeff slept peacefully enough in the one spare room the ranch-house possessed, taking care however to keep his guns within reach. Now and again he awakened — due, he imagined, to his strange surroundings — and sat listening intently, but no sound disturbed the infinite quiet of the prairie night.

The following morning, the moment breakfast was finished, he insisted on taking the girl for a ride.

'To where?' she asked in surprise, pausing in the midst of clearing the table. 'Riding is about the last thing I have time for when I've so many things to do about the house.'

'They can wait this time,' Jeff told her. 'I want you to come with me up into the mountains — if you can trust me, that is?'

'Trust you?' She looked at him with her frank violet eyes. 'Of course I can trust you.'

'Thanks.' Jeff smiled. 'That means a lot to me. Anyway, once we've gotten to Demon's Head Pass I'll explain why this ranch of yours isn't nearly as dead as you think.'

'You get goin',' the girl's father said, nodding. 'I'll do the clearin' away.'

'Okay,' the girl shrugged.

She followed Jeff out on to the porch, then led the way round to the stables. As on the previous evening she was again in her working outfit of cotton shirt and blue levis, her blonde hair flowing free.

'Suppose,' she asked, as she and Jeff saddled their horses, 'Poker should happen to see us and start some funny business? I wouldn't put it past him.'

Jeff patted his .45s. 'These aren't for decoration,' he replied. 'Just the same if you're scared I reckon we can call the whole thing off — '

'Scared?' Her violet eyes challenged him. 'Who's scared?'

Jeff grinned and said no more, satisfied that his 'dare' had been sufficient. Side by side he and the girl rode away from the ranch and across the dusty pasture land in the blazing sunlight. Jeff rode with a very deliberate slowness, apparently because he wanted to view the scenery. In a sense this was correct, but the scenery was not inanimate. He liked the vision of the girl beside him, fresh and youthful, every line of her strong young figure carved out in brilliance by the glare of the morning sun. Whether or not she sensed his scrutiny he did not know, but now and again he caught the ghost of an amused smile about her mouth.

'That's Poker's spread in the far distance,' she said. 'The Lazy-Y. You can see for yourself how nicely the water is doing for him.'

'Yeah.' Jeff mused for a moment and then said, 'He'd better use it whilst he can, too, for I'm thinkin' he isn't goin' to have it to use for much longer.'

Then presently she indicated the opposite end of the valley which Jeff had noticed in the twilight the previous evening.

The girl gave him a curious glance but he did not explain further. Together they jogged their mounts onwards, pausing at last when they had finished the long, dusty climb which brought them to the tumbling stream in Demon's Head Pass where Jeff had stopped the previous evening.

'Okay,' he said, dropping from his saddle. 'This is where we start to look around.'

He lifted the girl down from her mount and then grinned at her indignant expression as his hands remained supporting her under the arms. She drew free of his grip quickly.

'I'm not exactly unaccustomed to getting off a horse,' she exclaimed impatiently.

'No, sure yore not — but just the

same you might have slipped. As I said last night, I always like to help a lady — Anyway,' Jeff added, changing the subject, 'take a look. See what you make of it and then tell me.'

The girl followed the direction he indicated and stood gazing at the tumbling, frothing water which was cascading past them, boiling upwards from some source deep underground. For quite a while she remained motionless, just looking.

'Well, so what?' she questioned, puzzled. 'This is the stream which used to irrigate our pastures until the avalanche changed its course and gave Poker the benefit. I've seen it all before. I'm afraid I can't see what good it does to look at it again.'

'You can't, eh? I'll tell you. Your dad said that he couldn't claim this water because an 'Act of God' has changed its course — which means that Poker can't claim it either if it's taken away from him. You get the idea? He's no more entitled to it than your dad is. Whoever gets it can keep it, and no legal strings attached.'

The girl's puzzled expression deepened. 'Well, I — I can see what you mean but — It isn't possible to get this stream back. Look at the toughness and height of these damming walls — and even if they could be blasted away there's no guarantee that the stream would flow in the right direction. So taking it all round I just can't see what you're driving at.'

'I wasn't thinkin' of blasting.' Jeff studied the stream for several moments, his keen eyes glancing about the rugged terrain. 'I was thinkin',' he finished, 'of a pipeline. I'm a mining engineer, remember, and such projects fall just naturally into my territory.'

'A pipeline?' the girl repeated, starting. 'Why, you mean like the pipes they sometimes use for oil when it has to go over difficult terrain?'

'Uh-huh — and what I don't know about pipelines isn't worth the knowin', I reckon. You get the idea, don't you?

The entrance to the pipeline would be here.'

'I don't want to sound dense but I'm afraid I don't understand.'

Jeff smiled. 'Okay — and you're not dense, either. Makes a difference with me 'cos I know my subject. What I mean is, the entrance to the pipeline here would be in the form of a culvert. This water would rush into it — but instead of it carryin' on and plunging down into the far end of the valley, where Poker would get all the benefit, it would be diverted so's it came to your end of the valley — an' there's no law Poker can invoke to stop it since the water isn't legally his.'

A glow had come to the pretty girl's face.

'Why, that's wonderful!' she cried. 'And one of the simplest ideas out, too! I don't know why on earth dad or I didn't think of it ourselves.'

'Hardly likely you would, Miss Kemp. It's the sort of notion that only occurs to a minin' engineer — an' a fast thinker,' Jeff added, his jaw tightening.

Babs' eyes turned to him. 'A fast thinker? Meaning yourself?'

'Meanin' Poker Barrow! Why do you suppose he suddenly offered to buy your spread? Generosity of nature? Not a bit of it! It was because he must have been up here and figgered out an idea similar to mine — a pipeline system. In that way he probably aimed to water both his own and your spread — when he'd bought it — and double his output and income. Two minds thinkin' alike, an' that's why I stopped your dad sellin'. I just had to, don't you see?'

'And we jumped all over you for it,' the girl sighed. 'I'm sorry, Mr Alroyd — really I am.'

'The name's Jeff,' he grinned, 'an' there's nothin' to be sorry for . . . However,' he continued, becoming serious again, 'to just decide that we need a pipeline isn't the be-all and end-all by a long shot. We've got to have everythin' legal else we're liable to be stymied.'

'Meanin'?'

'Well, this stream f'instance. Where it goes doesn't concern anybody, but it must be owned at its source by somebody.'

'It sure is,' a voice remarked drily. 'The State!'

Jeff and the girl swung round. They had been so concentrated on studying the stream, its noise drowning all other sounds, that they had failed to hear the approaching hoofs of a solitary horseman. Now they saw Poker Barrow himself leaning on the saddle-horn of his massive sorrel. He was regarding them in dour amusement, his black stetson pushed on the back of his head. He flicked away a smouldering cigarette from between his fingers.

'Don't mind me keeping a check on your movements, do you?' he enquired. 'After last night, stranger, I sort of figgered I'd better keep a bead on you — just in case you happened to get too much in my way.'

The girl gave Barrow a look of consternation and then came forward.

'Then you must have heard all that we've been saying?'

'Most of it.' Barrow grinned down at Babs. 'Certainly enough for me to gather the drift of what's comin'. An' I've got to hand it to this stranger: he knows his way around. You guessed my aim nicely, feller,' he added to Jeff. 'A pipeline. That's just what I'm intendin' to use.'

'You mean you did,' Jeff retorted. 'You'll not get the chance now.'

'No?' Barrow grinned all the more. 'That depends on which of us has the most money an' which can ride the fastest to Stirling City — which is a considerable distance to the north. There ain't no train there until evenin' and I don't propose to wait that long . . . As to money, I don't think there's much doubt as to who's got the most; and as far as ridin' goes I'll back this sorrel of mine against any cayuse you've got.'

'I don't get it,' Jeff said, frowning.

'It's simple enough. This stream is

owned by the State — and neither you nor me can interfere with it unless we own it. A change of course by natural cause don't come into it. To own it means paying the State for a claim on it, and that claim has to be paid in Stirling City where the nearest authorities are located. I thought I'd make sure first if you had any ideas about a pipeline before I paid out, so I've kept my eye on you. Now I'm satisfied, and right now I'm headin' for Stirling City to buy this stream from under your nose! If you think you c'n stop me you'd better start revisin' your notions.'

Poker spurred his horse abruptly. The animal reared, swung round and then bore the rancher swiftly down the rocky declivity where the stream had once plunged. Jeff stared after him with grim eyes.

'Nice work,' he muttered. 'Doesn't seem to be much doubt about it that Poker Barrow knows his way around.'

'But what do we do?' the girl asked anxiously. 'If he stakes a claim first, Jeff, we're finished. It will stop us making any legal alteration in the stream and we'll just have to sell out to him, and he knows it.'

'Don't I know it too,' Jeff muttered, thinking swiftly. 'He's right about money, too. It won't be possible to buy a stake in this stream without a fair amount of cash — Look, I've got a thousand dollars in a Kansas bank which I can draw on, and a cheque book in my pocket. I'm willin' to sink the lot in this gamble. That's the measure of how much faith I have in it. How much can you and your dad provide?'

'Well, I — ' The girl hesitated, reflecting, and for a moment Jeff fancied he caught a faint hint of distrust.

'I've got to know,' he insisted. 'I can hold the claim with a thousand if I can get to Stirling first; but I must know how much more I can supply to complete the deal.'

'As far as I'm aware dad should be

good for about five thousand dollars,' the girl answered quickly, apparently casting all hesitation on one side as the urgency of the situation struck home to her. 'And I've another two thousand I can call on, left me by an uncle — '

'Right!' Jeff swung into the saddle of his mare. 'That's all I need to know. Eight thousand dollars between us. That should do. You find your own way back home, Babs: I'm goin' to beat Poker to Stirling if it's the last thing I do.'

He spurred his mare and she darted forward. He looked back with a smile.

'Don't mind me calling you Babs!' he yelled, as he saw the girl waving after him. 'We might as well start to get properly acquainted . . . '

★ ★ ★

Once he had left the valley behind Jeff had the open mesa before him, which after a while shaded off into the endless yellow of the sun-blistered desert. It

46

was when he reached it that he obtained his first glimpse of Poker Barrow, infinitely far ahead, a fast-moving black dot in the midst of the rolling wastes of sand, scrub, and occasional cactus outcroppings which scarred the waste.

Jeff smiled to himself. He wondered how prepared Poker was for the long journey to Stirling City across miles of arid wilderness. He himself had water and provisions in the saddle bag, left there from his journeying the previous day. He also knew that there are limits to what horseflesh can stand in the torrid sunlight; and in this blank, merciless expanse there were few waterholes which were not rank poison. Definitely, the going was not too promising.

'I reckon we'll let him exhaust himself, Smoky,' Jeff murmured to the mare. 'Floggin' his beast at that rate it'll give out under him afore he's gotten half way. He's that plumb anxious about everythin' he seems to have forgotten that little point.'

He continued his own fairly leisurely pace across the wilderness, the sunlight searing into his back and shoulders, the sweat gleaming on Smoky's glossy sides as she trotted on gamely. She was a tough animal, well fed, and accustomed to many a hard ride . . . So, gradually, after nearly two hours of steady going, the distant dot which was Poker had come perceptibly nearer, and he was moving much more slowly.

Jeff dismounted, watered his horse, and then took a long drink for himself. He squinted briefly at the sun to judge the time and decided it was close on noon. He waited another ten minutes or so then patted the rested mare's nose.

'This is where we get him, lady,' he murmured. 'He's kept that cayuse of his goin' non-stop since he started and there isn't any horseflesh livin' as can stand up to that . . . Okay, let's overtake.'

Smoky pawed the dusty sand and

with a grin Jeff swung into the saddle and touched the animal's withers with his spurs. Understanding what was required of her, and refreshed after her rest, Smoky burst into a hurtling dash of speed as Jeff gave her her head. Far away, the toiling, plodding horse of Poker — with him in the saddle — became clearer; and clearer still. In twenty minutes he was within shooting distance.

As the thunder of speeding hoofs beat upon his ears he turned in sudden consternation. Then he sat half twisted in the saddle, watching blankly as Jeff came racing up.

'See you in Stirling!' Jeff called to him, and went hurtling past in a cloud of grains.

Barrow stared after him menacingly and dug his spurs into the exhausted sorrel's sides. For a moment it served to increase the jogtrot to a run, then the animal fell back again. It had about reached the limit of its endurance.

'Too lazy, huh?' Barrow snapped.

'Okay, I reckon there are other ways of stoppin' that smart jigger — '

He whipped out his right-hand .38, took aim at the fleeing figure of Jeff, and fired. Jeff, concentrating on his riding, was suddenly aware of the report and then a slicing, tearing pain across the top of his head as his hat went flying. Dazed, he reeled sideways and fell from the saddle into the sand. Smoky wheeled round, whinneyed, and came trotting back towards him. For a moment or two Jeff lay where he was, too completely dazed to think straight.

'The dirty, no-account — ' Jeff breathed, and staggered to his feet, his hand to his head. No blood had been drawn. Evidently the bullet had whizzed straight across the top of his skull without breaking the skin, and the impact had momentarily stunned him. He picked up his hat and jammed it back on as Barrow came riding up with his .38 still levelled.

'So you want to play the game the hard way, huh?' Jeff snapped, squinting up at him in the sun glare.

'I don't care which way I play it, Alroyd, just as long as I get to Stirling City before you do,' Barrow answered. 'I'm not aimin' to kill you: that'd make things tough for me with the sheriff — but I'll wing you if I have to. I reckon the best thing I can do is take your horse along with me. If that doesn't cramp your style I don't know what will.'

Jeff breathed hard. The .38 was still cocked on him — and it remained on him as Barrow clicked his teeth and automatically caused Smoky to come over to him. He reached out and grasped the reins. The animal shied restlessly as she sensed that she was in other hands than those of her master.

'I reckon it's more'n fifty miles back home,' Poker said dryly. 'Give my love to Babs when you land — if you do. As you're pretty likely to find out, the desert isn't much of a place for a walk without plenty of water.'

'Love him, Smoky,' Jeff called, with a

faint grin — and Barrow, preparing to move on frowned down on him.

'What did you say?'

Jeff did not answer and a second later Barrow found out the meaning of the request. Smoky, under orders, nestled her big head up against Barrow's arm and diverted his gun hand. Instantly Jeff sprang, whipped the gun away, and by sheer strength pulled the cursing, struggling man from the saddle and down into the sand. His remaining gun was whipped from him before he even had a chance to grasp what was happening.

'Okay!' he said savagely, struggling to his feet. 'So you want it your way! Get busy and shoot me then. I reckon I can't stop you when I've no guns!'

'All I'm anxious to do is keep you away from Stirling until I get there,' Jeff answered, flinging the gun away over his shoulder. 'There are two ways of doing it. One is to take your horse three miles further on and leave it there for you to find — and the other is to work

something out of my system, something
which has been seizin' me up far too
long for my liking.'

'Meaning what?' Barrow demanded.

'My dislike of you. Meanin' this,
f'rinstance — '

Jeff's right fist bunched and slammed
forward, landing under Barrow's jaw.
He stumbled backwards, recovered, and
lashed out an uppercut. It took Jeff on
the chest, but he was braced for it. A
left pistoned into Barrow's stomach,
doubling him: a short-armed jab
straightened him again but, winded and
dazed, he dropped gasping into the
sand. Dully he half scrambled into a
sitting position and shook his head
stupidly from side to side.

'I'd like to do more,' Jeff said bitterly,
'but I haven't got the time. Perhaps I'll
have the pleasure later!'

He whirled into Smoky's saddle,
snatched the reins of Barrow's horse,
and kept the animal beside him until he
reckoned that the stipulated three miles
had been covered. Here he released the

sorrel and then glanced back. He grinned faintly at the vision of the distant speck in the shimmering desert heat which betokened Poker making slow and laborious progress in the burning sun — then relieved of the brake the sorrel had been on her Smoky was given her head and raced northwards, Jeff well satisfied that he would be an easy first into Stirling City.

He was right. It was late afternoon when he finally arrived there. The city was a fairly busy one, a sprawling outgrowth of the western desert in which was centred most of the law and order for two hundred miles around. His business with the authorities took him half an hour and he emerged from the official headquarters looking fairly pleased with himself.

'Well, I reckon that's that,' he murmured to Smoky, as she stood nodding sleepily at the tie-rack. 'You an' me need a rest, lady, before we start back. Leastways you do . . . See you again later.'

He patted the mare's nose affection-
ately and then began a slow walk down
the boardwalk of the main street,
glancing about him as he went. He
passed the sheriff's office, a saloon, a
general stores, an assayer's; and then
just beyond the town's big livery stable
he came to the place he wanted: On the
broad window it said Thorne &
Billings, Mining Engineers. He nodded
to himself and went in, to find himself
in a small boxed-in enquiry office.

There was the sound of movement
from behind the plywood partitioning
and then a man in shirtsleeves
appeared and looked over steel-
rimmed glasses. There was about him
a general air of not wanting to be
bothered.

'Afternoon, stranger,' he greeted.
'Somethin' I can do for you?'

'You can. I want an estimate — that
is if you do any deals in pipelines?'

'Sure do. For oil, you mean?'

'Not this time.' Jeff shook his head.

'Then I don't reckon I can help you

much. Who in tarnation ever heard of pipelines bein' used for anything 'cept oil?'

'I'm aimin' to use mine for water,' Jeff explained calmly. 'I'll need pipeline to cover about three miles, and the labour to build it. Be a plenty tough job with a lot of rock to be blasted before we can sink the supports . . . ' Jeff pushed up his hat on his forehead and spread his hands. 'That's the set-up. I can't provide the labour and materials, but if you can I'll — '

'Sure I can,' the man interrupted, 'but it'll cost you plenty. Where's the line to be?'

'D'you know Double Peak Valley?'

The man reflected. 'Double Peak Valley . . . ? Yeah, I think I do. Across the desert to the south of here — near the Apache Mountains?'

'That's it.'

'Mmmm.' The man compressed his lips and leaned his forearms on the counter. 'That's the tough part,' he said, shaking his head. 'There's no way of sendin' pipeline sections across th' desert. There'd only be a stage or a hoss for it, and the sections are too heavy for that. Railroad's the only way, goin' by Paint Rock and through Saba Mountain Cleft. I s'pose Double Peak has a railroad station? — or is it more cockeyed than I'm thinkin'?'

'Since Double Peak is a town of sorts I suppose it must have,' Jeff responded.

'Okay then. Stick around for a minute, pardner, while I work out the things for you — Three miles of line and labour to fix it, didn't yuh say?'

'That's it,' Jeff confirmed, 'but I'll supervise operations myself. I'm a mining engineer and I know what I want. You can leave out the expense of a foreman. I'll make a darned sight better one myself.'

The man nodded and vanished again behind the partition. Jeff rolled a cigarette, lighted it, and waited. There was a long interval, then after what had evidently been mathematical computations the man reappeared.

'I reckon a job like that couldn't be done under three thousand dollars,' he said. 'Includin' everything, that is — from start to finish. Labour, pipes, freight-charges . . . '

'That,' Jeff said slowly, 'takes thinkin' about. Three thousand dollars, eh? Well, thanks anyway. You'll be hearing from me.'

'Glad to — any time.'

Jeff strolled outside to the boardwalk and stood thinking. $3,000. Yet knowing what he did of mining engineering it was only what he expected. In this area the cost of freight was the biggest headache, and as far as he could see there was no possible way of circumventing it, either.

'Nothing much more I can do right now except get back to the Double Circle and see what old man Kemp and Babs have to say,' he mused, flicking away his cigarette, 'and the sooner the better. There's the heck of distance to cover.'

Decided, he began walking briskly

back to the spot where his mare still stood. He glanced about him as he went, half expecting to see some sign of Poker Barrow. Since he did not he assumed that, knowing that he could never stake his claim in the mountain stream, Barrow had given up the idea as a bad job and returned to Double Peak —

But in this Jeff was mistaken.

Barrow had finished the trip to Stirling City, and even as Jeff was glancing about him Barrow was watching from the narrow space between two wooden buildings, mounted on his weary horse. He continued watching until he saw Jeff mount his mare and then canter swiftly away down the street to hit the desert trail for home.

Grim-faced, Barrow urged his sorrel out of concealment and went across to the office of the mining engineers. Tethering his horse to the tie-rack he strode into the enquiry office and banged fiercely on the desk for attention. The man in the steel-rimmed spectacles appeared in a moment or two, looking curiously at the handsome-faced, travel-stained stranger and assessing his obvious urgency.

'You had a minin' engineer in here not long ago,' Barrow said briefly. 'He's a pardner of mine — What did he want? A pipeline estimate?'

'Mebby he did — mebby he didn't.' The eyes peered suspiciously over the spectacles. 'Think I should tell you?'

'Quit foolin' around!' Barrow snapped. 'I've got to be knowin'! No secret about it, is there?'

The mining engineer considered this and then shrugged. 'Well, no, I reckon there isn't. Matter of fact he did ask for an estimate and — '

'And what was your quote?'

'Three thousand dollars for three miles o' pipeline and labourers to build it.'

'Thanks!' Barrow grinned broadly. 'That's all I wanted to know — Except for one thing.' He hesitated. 'How do you figger sendin' that piping?'

'If he takes it on it'll go railroad. No other way to do it.'

'If he takes it on?' Barrow repeated. 'Y'mean he hasn't given you the go-ahead?'

The man shook his head. 'Nope. Said he'd have to think over the price. Lettin' me know later.'

'Well . . . Thanks.'

With a nod Barrow left the office. His grin was even broader as he stood thinking to himself and looking over the busy main street.

'So he didn't give the go-ahead,' he murmured. 'That means he must be short on the money side . . . He'll have to find it somehow, though. Mmmm — this is going to be interestin'!'

Still smiling to himself he stepped off the boardwalk and unfastened his sorrel from the hitch-rail.

3

Due to the fact that he had to rest his mare on several occasions during the return trip across the desert, it was after midnight when Jeff, wornout and dusty, at last arrived back at the Double Circle — and he arrived on foot, leading the mare beside him. For the last five miles she had been incapable of carrying his weight any longer.

To Jeff's satisfaction, old man Kemp and the girl were still up waiting for him. He put the exhausted mare in the stable, fed and watered her, and then went into the ranch house. A meal was waiting for him in the comfortable living room and the moment he had freshened up he tackled it avidly.

Both the old man and Babs let him eat in peace for the first five minutes, then their eyes began to aim questions. So Jeff began talking.

'At least the stream is our legal property,' he announced. 'I fixed that, with my own signature, so actually it is my property, but we won't argue over that — '

'How much did it cost to do that?' old man Kemp asked quietly.

'Seven thousand dollars — and I had to give my own cheque for one thousand to hold it, which cleans me out. But it makes it that nobody else can touch it — Poker for instance.'

'Then you beat him to it?' the girl exclaimed eagerly. 'I'm dying to know what happened!'

'Plenty happened.' Jeff grinned reflectively and related what had occurred, then he looked at the brooding face of old man Kemp.

'Seven thousand dollars . . . Ain't too sure I like the sound of that. It's a whale of a lot of kudos, son, for just one stream.'

'Mebby it is,' Jeff admitted, 'but I don't have to tell you that all watercourses rate high because they're life and death to a rancher. The fact remains I've bought it. Six thousand more dollars have to be found to finish off the deal — an' I've three days to do it in. So having got this far I'm waiting to see what you have to say about it.'

'We can do it,' Babs said, with quiet assurance. 'I've been explaining things to dad, and as I said he has five thousand he can use, and I've got two. So we'll still have a thousand in hand. As long as it stays that way we shan't have the awful feeling that we're completely without backing.'

'So we buy the stream,' her father said. 'And then what? It looks as though Poker'll go right on using it! Yes, yes, I know about the pipeline,' he added, as Jeff looked at him, 'but where do we get the money to build that? An' it's the only way in which a stream can be forced on to our land. We could dam it up I suppose, now we own it, and stop it flowin' down to Poker, but that wouldn't guarantee that we'd get it. It might flow just any place! Water doesn't know any master, 'less it's in a pipe like yore intendin'. An' even if we dammed it I wouldn't put it past Poker to blow up the dam and claim it were an accident — an 'Act of God'. Then we'd be no nearer. That critter would do just anythin' I reckon.'

Jeff slowly put down his coffee cup. 'Since the answer's a pipeline, then that's what we're having!' he declared. 'I know what I've taken on and without much money to back me up, too. But we'll get through — Okay, so when the claim's paid for in full we have a thousand dollars left. Mmmm — that means we need a further two thousand dollars from some place.'

'For the pipeline?' old man Kemp questioned.

'That's right — and for labour and transit costs. Three thousand for all that. Then we're all set . . . '

Kemp got to his feet, musing uneasily. He aimed Jeff a grim glance.

'It looks to me, son, as though yore tryin' to start runnin' afore you can walk,' he said. 'Suppose you tell me how we're ever to get hold of two thousand dollars with a dyin' ranch all around us?'

'There's one way,' Jeff replied quietly, 'an' I didn't happen to just think of it now, either. Bin in my mind for some time. I mean — winning it.'

The girl gave a start and something like consternation crossed her pretty face.

'Great heavens, Jeff, you don't mean you'd gamble to try and get it?'

'Why not?' he asked bluntly. 'Or are you one of those gals who don't approve of it?'

'It's not that: I've nothing against gambling — and neither has dad. But for such a stake . . . And what do you use for money to start playing?'

'The thousand there will be left over when the stream claim is paid. I've got to turn that thousand into about five — or more — to put us on the comfortable side, and that's what I aim to do in the Twin Dollar tomorrow night. Naturally, I'm taking a chance, but since there never was a gamble without one, who cares?'

There was a long silence, then presently old man Kemp gave his low chuckle. Babs shot him a surprised look.

'Okay, son, you try it,' he exclaimed, grinning. 'Come to think of it I once won a herd o' cattle playin' poker. I was 'bout your age at the time. You'll win — if you know your way around with a deck of cards.'

'I'll win,' Jeff said, 'because I have to. There are no two ways about it. If I once get it into my head that I might lose I — ' He stopped and gave his genial smile. 'Forget it,' he said briefly. 'That's settled, then. Tomorrow you must mail the remainder of that money to Stirling City, and tomorrow night . . . Well!'

★   ★   ★

Jeff slept heavily all that night after his gruelling journey to and from Stirling

City. The next morning he went into town and mailed the additional money to Stirling City to complete the stream claim. Then feeling considerably relieved in his mind with that responsibility out of the way he returned to help the girl and her father with the heavier jobs about the ranch.

In the afternoon he settled himself down with a fairly worn deck of cards and until darkness he spent his time practising with them. Babs watching him interestedly, realised within the first few minutes that only a master could handle the cards the way he did.

'Where did you learn?' she finally asked him in surprise.

Jeff cascaded the pack from one hand to the other and grinned.

'Ever hear of 'Three Ace Alroyd'?' he asked — and over in the basket-chair by the window old man Kemp gave a sudden start of recollection.

'Say, I did!' he ejaculated. 'Way back in the old days — an' I never knew a guy like him. I once saw him come out

with three straight flushes in succession
— Alroyd!' he broke off. 'I knew I'd
heard the name some place. You related
to him?'

'He was my father,' Jeff responded.
'Died two years ago — th' old buzzard!
Hard drinker, tough hitter, and a born
gambler. He drove my mother to the
grave thirty years ahead of her time.'
Jeff meditated for a moment and then
his mood lightened. 'He taught me
everythin' there is to know about cards.
When I've got to play for money I play
— otherwise I'm just not interested.
Outside of makin' money it's a mug's
game.'

''Three Ace' Alroyd's boy,' Kemp
breathed, a new light in his eyes. 'Well,
I'll be dog-goned! That sure makes one
helluva difference! I reckon there's
nobody I'd sooner have around this
ranch.'

Jeff's eyes strayed to the girl and her
gaze averted to the trifle she was sewing.

'You feel that way too, Babs?' he
asked levelly.

'I — I sort of feel safe when you're around anyway,' she replied evasively, and in spite of herself she coloured. 'And I might as well admit that that's more than I ever felt concerning Poker.'

'Oh, you're safe enough,' Jeff assured her, 'an' it's been worth coming here if only to meet you and chase Poker away . . . ' He suddenly motioned to the girl. 'Here — come an' sit beside me. I'll show you some tricks. You never know when you may need 'em.'

'But Jeff, I couldn't possibly — '

''Course you could! Bring up a chair!'

Babs smiled faintly and then complied. The nearness of her, and the necessity to grasp her slim hands and show her how to handle the cards, could have meant plain nothing to judge from the expression on Jeff's face — but deep down he was thrilling to every moment of it.

In between whiles he studied the girl's pretty face thoughtfully — the straightness of her nose, the firmness of her young figure, her readiness to laugh every time she made a mistake. He found it increasingly hard to keep his mind on the job of showing her the card tricks, but somehow he managed to preserve his air of detachment. His emotions only found expression in a few words when the girl had mastered three tricks.

'To think,' he muttered, 'that guy Poker might have corralled you for himself if I hadn't stepped in. It makes me hate him a darned sight more'n I do already!'

'I'm glad you . . . stepped in,' the girl said, and looked at him frankly.

He hesitated. It was a moment when everything was set fair for him to kiss her — and he had a sneaking suspicion that she would not have resisted, either. Then he refrained and got to his feet instead.

'It's been nice showin' you, Babs,' he murmured, patting her shapely arm. 'Now I'd better start dolling myself up a bit before I take 'em for a ride in the Twin Dollar.'

He left the room to make his

preparations and when, towards eight in the evening, he entered the gambling saloon through the batwings he found — as he had expected — that the place was at the zenith of the activity. He stood for a moment, hands on hips, wrinkling his nose at the change of atmosphere.

It stank of liquor, strong tobacco, and perspiring bodies. The faro and roulette tables were busy, there was a rattle of poker chips. Far away in the haze, in a corner amidst forlorn looking palms, an 'orchestra' of guitars and a tin-panny piano strummed valiantly.

The tables were filled — punchers, store keepers, one or two half-breeds, some Mexicans, and a number of loosely dressed women whose fading charms had been given a fillip by cosmetics and hair dye.

Jeff strolled over to the bar and ordered a whisky. As he stood drinking it his eyes studied the scene reflected by the back-bar mirror. Presently his slow grin appeared as his wandering gaze detected somebody he had hoped to meet — Poker Barrow. He was at a distant table, lounging back in his chair with cards in his hands and a half-filled glass on the table at his side.

'Couldn't be better,' Jeff murmured. 'Sort of makes things even to take Poker for all he's got . . . '

He finished his drink, then with his thumbs latched casually on his cross-over gun-belts he strolled over to where Barrow sat playing. Barrow's dark eyes glanced up and then back to his cards.

'I thought snakes went to cover at night,' he commented, and the three men with whom he was playing grinned broadly among themselves.

'You sort of give the lie to that, don't you?' Jeff asked calmly.

Barrow looked up again, his eyes narrowed.

'What in tarnation d'you want, anyway?' he demanded. 'Since yore evidently too plain dumb to know it, yore puttin' me off my game.'

'It's not me that's doin' that, Poker;

it's more likely it's because you don't know how to play it.'

'Who? Me?' Barrow grinned widely. 'Well, if that ain't just the sort of loco remark I might have expected from a guy like you!'

'How's about you an' me playin' a game — just ourselves?' Jeff asked. 'You think you can play poker — Well, so do I, I reckon.'

Barrow stopped playing and sat back in his chair.

'Well, I ain't so sure about that . . . ' He threw his cards on the table and pondered; then finally he jerked his head to the three men with him.

'Blow!' he ordered — and tossing their cards down they got up; but they did not go far. They stood waiting to see what happened next. Other men and women had drifted nearer too — interested. In all his career as a poker player Barrow had never been challenged to a game, and by a comparative stranger, too.

'You show sense,' Jeff remarked dryly.

He sat down at the opposite side of the table and cuffed his hat on to his forehead. Then he picked up the scattered cards and went through them carefully.

'I reckon we'll have a fresh deck,' he decided, and as Barrow merely shrugged one of the punchers went and brought one. Jeff took it, examined it, tore off the wrapper, and then put the deck on the table.

'What's the ante?' Barrow asked. 'Five cents? I can't see you affordin' much more.'

'You can't, eh? Five hundred dollars to start with . . . ' and Jeff moved his chips into position.

'Five hundred?' Barrow stared. 'Yore crazier than I figgered! What's the idea?'

'What d'you care? Can't you match it?'

Barrow put his chips on the table to five hundred equivalent and his dark eyes were frankly suspicious.

'I get it,' he said finally. 'You want to buy that pipeline, eh? And this is the only way you can think of to do it. Feller, you just don't know what yore gettin' into!'

Jeff shuffled the cards and then plonked them down. 'Deal!' he ordered.

Barrow did so, five cards to himself and five to Jeff, then both men sat back to consider their hands. He discarded one card, Jeff two.

'Eight hundred,' Jeff said at length, and pushed over his own chips. The watchers waited

'Nine,' Barrow countered. Steadily the ante rose.

'I'm seein' yuh,' Barrow said, matching Jeff's bid. Jeff put his cards on the table — three cards of the same rank, and a pair. Barrow looked at them and grinned, then threw down a fours.

'Your bad luck, Alroyd,' he commented dryly. 'I'm staking all this, plus another five hundred.'

'Okay, stake how you like,' Jeff responded, and moved his chips. 'Two hundred.'

The cards were dealt. Jeff pondered

his hand. There was something wrong somewhere. From his permutating of cards he knew he should have won that last trick — but somehow Barrow had managed to go one trick higher.

'Did you give my love to Babs like I told you?' Barrow asked after a moment, studying his cards.

'At the moment,' Jeff said quietly, 'everything is going along nicely — so I reckon we can leave Miss Kemp out of it if things are to stay that way.'

'I don't. She's the only gal around here who's worth lookin' at. Anyways, what's a gal for if you can't — '

Jeff's calm deserted him. There was something about Barrow's voice, about the words he had been intending to use which blinded Jeff's reason for a moment. He leapt up, half overturning the table, and slammed his fist with devastating force into Barrow's sneering face. With a choking gasp he toppled backwards in his chair and crashed to the floor.

'Next time you mention Babs Kemp,

keep it clean,' Jeff panted, glaring down. 'Mebby that will fix your dirty mouth for you! If you've got to find somebody to pick on you can — '

Jeff stopped, amazement crossing his face. Barrow's hand had made a dive at several cards which had spewed from his jacket sleeve in his fall. Jeff was there first, whipping them up. The backs were identical to the pack in use.

'Duplicates — !' Jeff reached out and dragged the dazed gambler to his feet. 'Why, you dirty heel, no wonder you can win poker if this is how you play it! Your man brought a prepared deck, huh? Identical with these.'

'What the hell are you — '

'Save the excuses!' Jeff flung the cards away and whipped out his gun. 'I thought there was somethin' crooked someplace! Most men would ha' given you a slug in the belly for this, but I ain't aimin' to do that. Instead I'm goin' to take you for all you've got! Sit down — and start playing the game straight. That is, if y'know how!'

Jeff kicked Barrow's chair round and righted it. Then he gave the gambler a shove so that he fell into it.

Grim-faced, Jeff settled down opposite him, his gun on the table beside him ready for instant use. Though he knew he was surrounded by Barrow's own trigger-men — and therefore enemies of himself — he also knew that the great preponderance of men and women in the saloon were dead set against a crooked gambler. In that, he realised, lay his strength.

'Deal!' he snapped, and slammed down the deck. 'An' we start again — even!' He sorted out the chips. 'Five hundred as before.'

Barrow added his own chips, and from then on the onlookers watched a game such as they had never seen before. As each hand was called, Jeff went a trick higher. He beat one pair with two; triplets with a straight; a flush with a full; and finally fours with a straight flush. Only then did he stop and commence to reckon up.

'Eight thousand dollars you owe me, Barrow,' he announced. 'Better make it good right now — an' I'm not talkin' about a cheque, either!'

'It's no use sayin' that,' Barrow retorted. 'I haven't got that much money here!'

'Then you'd best get. I'm not leavin' without it — an' neither are you. You know me well enough by now to have figgered that I'm not the kind of guy who talks for the sake of it.'

Barrow hesitated and then motioned into the distance. A man with a white shirt and glossy dark hair — the saloon owner — came towards him, bent low to listen to the words whispered in his ear. He nodded and went away. Presently he returned with eight $1,000 notes and handed them over. Savagely Barrow hurled them across the table.

'Thanks,' Jeff murmured, pocketing them. He holstered his gun and straightened his hat.

'You'll be hearin' from me, Alroyd!' Barrow told him venomously. 'Don't think you can get away with this! There isn't a guy livin' who can take me for a hay ride and get away with it!'

'I played straight — and so did you once you'd seen your mistake,' Jeff retorted. 'Don't think I didn't guess that you were tryin' to stop me buyin' my pipeline. And don't try any funny business in future, Barrow, either! I'm warnin' you! If other fellows are afraid of you I'm not . . . 'Night!'

Jeff gave a grim smile and turned to push his way through the crowd.

4

The delight of old man Kemp and the girl at learning of Jeff's success was ample compensation for the concentrated ordeal of playing through which he had passed — controlling his fingers and watching any false moves of Barrow's at the same time . . . He went to bed happy, and the next morning set off by railroad for Stirling City and there settled matters with the mining engineers.

Within a week the first pipes began to arrive and Jeff and the girl found themselves busy with the buckboard and team, transferring the pipes from the railroad station in Double Peak to the ranch. Jeff had no fears about the pipe sections being interfered with. They were too heavy to be smashed in silence, or to be stolen — so he stacked them in one of the ranch's spare outhouses. Even so he slept each night with a gun close at hand and one ear cocked even in sleep for signs of sabotage. Knowing how Poker Barrow felt about things, Jeff was prepared for the possibility that the gambler might try one mighty explosion and destroy the pipes that way.

In a fortnight all of the sections had arrived, together with the necessary wooden scaffolding props and a squad of twelve powerful labourers who took over the bunkhouse which had formerly been used by the Double Circle's outfit.

Within twenty days from when he had been beaten at poker, Barrow was treated to the disturbing sight — as he watched events one morning from high up in the Apache Range — of a gang of a dozen husky men, supervised by Jeff, as they set to work erecting the first props and transferring the rocks which would ultimately dam the water to his own pasture land.

Barrow tried by every twist of his imagination to think of a way to circumvent the disaster happening before his eyes, but no foolproof notion seemed to present itself. Finally, mainly in desperation, he went to his lawyer in Double Peak.

'There's got to be some way to stop them, Ezra!' he insisted. 'If they get away with this my pasture'll be drier than a bush fire. I reckon that in a week they'll cut off the water and start testin' it through the first length of pipeline. Certainly it wont take 'em long now.'

Ezra Billings, Double Peak's oldest lawyer — and as straight a shooter as any — reflected for several minutes, stroking his tufty eyebrows.

'Well, I don't rightly see . . . ' He started speaking slowly and then stopped, his eyes fixed on the big relief map of the district on the opposite walls. 'Leastways, mebby I don't,' he amended, getting to his feet.

He wandered across to the map and stood surveying it critically. Barrow got up and crossed to his side. The lawyer glanced at him.

'Where does the pipe start?' he asked, and Barrow put his fingers on the spot.

'And finishes here,' he added, indicating the valley and then the square which was the Double Circle ranch.

The lawyer reflected. 'An he's comin' straight down from the mountains? No twists or turns?'

'None. He's starting where the stream first comes up from below . . .' A gleam came into Barrow's dark eyes. 'Why? Think you c'n do something, Ezra?'

'Tell you in a minute.' The lawyer rubbed his chin. 'I've got an idea workin' at the back of my mind and if things are as I think they are we might . . .'

He stopped talking and moved across to the bookcase, pulling forth a heavy tome on local and State Law. For nearly ten minutes he waded through it, thumbing the pages whilst Barrow watched impatiently.

'Come on, come on!' Barrow burst out at last. 'What gives?'

'I thought there was somethin'!' The lawyer snapped his fingers suddenly. 'Here it is! In between the source of that stream — an' the pipeline — and the finish of it, as it will be when the pipeline's completed, there's a strip of territory three miles long and a quarter of a mile wide, running parallel with the valley — See here! It's in the early map before any ranches were built.'

Barrow looked at the scale map and the date of 1860 beneath it. He nodded urgently.

'So?' he asked.

'All the land within that square is owned by the trustees of — er — ' More pages flipped. 'The trustees of Caleb Valson. He was a gold prospector in 1860. He staked a claim on that strip of land, thinkin' there was gold on it. There wasn't.'

'Well, what about it?' Barrow asked irritably. 'For Pete's sake, man, come to the point. What's the set up?'

'The set up,' the lawyer replied, 'is that Caleb never revoked the claim

— you can read all about it here — and on his death that strip of land went into the control of his trustees. Nobody ever bothered about a stream flowing across it towards the Double Circle — but they could h' done had they wanted. Now it's different, there being a pipeline — '

'I get it!' Barrow exclaimed. 'You mean that in crossing that strip of territory Alroyd is trespassing?'

'Yeah.' Billings put the book on one side. 'Which means he has either got to buy that strip of land so he can go over it in peace with his pipeline — else he's got to detour for three miles. That is one an' a half one way and one an' a half back to bring the pipe into a straight line again. A U-bend. That might make things kind of difficult for him.'

Barrow sat down slowly and pondered, then presently he began to smile.

'An' that will also cost him plenty of money,' he murmured. 'An' if he gets some more pipin' there are ways of dealin' with him.'

Ezra Billings spread his hands. 'That's up to you, Barrow. What do you want me to do? But it'd better not be anythin' dirty. I never touched a dirty deal in my life, and I don't aim to start now.'

Barrow said briefly: 'Get in touch with the trustees of that land strip, Ezra, and buy it for me. I don't care what the price is just as long as you get it.'

The lawyer nodded. 'Okay, Poker, I reckon that shouldn't be too difficult. Leave it to me.'

'I will — and the moment you have some news let me know. Then I'll give Mr Bright Boy Alroyd one hell of a shock!'

★ ★ ★

Jeff Alroyd stood on a high eminence of rock overlooking the site of the pipeline activities. He grinned to himself and drew the back of his hand over his streaming forehead. It was morning, three weeks after the commencement of the pipeline building, and to the din of the labouring men, the sullen beat of pile-drivers, the clank of shovels and staccato of picks, was added the clouds of dust pouring into the drenching heat of the Arizona sunlight.

'Three more weeks of this, Babs, and we'll have finished the job,' Jeff commented in satisfaction.

The girl standing beside him in her conventional working outfit, nodded eagerly. Throughout the past three weeks she had been constantly at his side, helping in smaller duties, seeing to it that foodstuffs and water were in plentiful supply.

'I just wander how Poker is taking it?' she murmured with a reflective smile.

'Who in heck cares?' Jeff snorted. 'He's beaten, an' he knows it — otherwise he'd ha' done plenty by this time . . . ' He took his eyes from the scene of workmanlike activity to look at her. Then he gave a start. 'Say,' he murmured, 'you may not know it, but you've more dirt on your face than a miner! Here — !' He whipped the handkerchief from her shirt pocket. 'Damp it.'

Babs obeyed and stood as passive as a little girl whilst he wiped the smudges away. Finally he stood back and considered the result.

'That's better,' he smiled, handing back the handkerchief. The girl gazed at him for a moment and then her eyes lowered shyly. 'And I want to thank you for being such a mighty help to me in these past weeks, Babs,' Jeff continued. 'An' I also reckon that any man who's got a gal like you beside him doesn't need to ask for much more.'

She smiled, her violet eyes bright in the sunlight.

'You seem to take an awfully long time to come round to realising it,' she remarked.

Jeff hesitated — then suddenly his arms were about her slender body, half raising her from her feet as he kissed her. Just as abruptly he released her and gave an awkward grin, smoothing his big hands down the side of his rough trousers.

'Sorry,' he muttered. 'I suppose I shouldn't ha' done that. I'm not the Poker type, y'know.'

'I know — otherwise I'd have kicked your shins.' The girl patted his arm gently. 'You don't have to — '

'So it's gotten around to neckin' has it?'

Babs, her sentence interrupted, swung round — as did Jeff beside her. He and the girl stood looking at the tall, rangy form of Barrow nearby. With him was the broad, tubby figure of Sheriff Hollows. Behind the men, nibbling at the sparse roots, were their horses.

'I thought I knew the voice,' Jeff growled, his jaw hardening.

''Bout time you did,' Barrow commented cynically.

'What's the matter, sheriff?' the girl asked deliberately, ignoring Barrow as his eyes went over her. 'I suppose it must be something pretty important or you wouldn't be here?'

'My business isn't with you, Miss Kemp,' the Sheriff answered. 'It's with the legal owner of this pipeline —Which'll be you Mr Alroyd, won't it? Yore Jeffrey Alroyd?'

'Sure I am,' Jeff responded, shrugging. 'What's that got to do with it?'

'Just had to verify it, that's all.' The sheriff handed over a foolscap-sized document, folded three times. 'This is an injunction issued by the Stirling authorities,' he explained. 'It restrains you from crossing this strip of land just here . . . ' And he indicated it.

Jeff stared blankly and exchanged a look with the girl; then he glanced through the document with her also reading it over his shoulder.

'Well, of all the cheap, low-down tricks!' she ejaculated finally, her eyes glinting as she swung on Barrow. 'You've dug up an ancient land right from somewheres and decided to enforce it!'

'Sure,' he agreed calmly. 'An' there's nothin' you or this dashin' stranger can do about it, either! If you don't take three quarters of your pipeline to bits and detour round this strip I've bought I'll take steps to make you!'

Jeff folded the document, his face bitter. He glanced at the sheriff.

'This in order, sheriff?'

'I guess so,' Hollows confirmed. 'Later in the day I'll be back with men to peg out the exact area where you can't cross. You've only two alternatives, Alroyd — to dismantle the pipe to the edge of the strip, and then detour round it: or else buy the strip from Barrow here.'

'An' I'm not aimin' to sell,' Barrow grinned. 'An' nothin' you can think of 'll make me!'

'No, I don't expect it will,' Jeff told him sourly.

'A fine no-account heel you turned out to be!' Babs exclaimed, and stood for a moment breathing stormily; then she flung herself away in disgust so that her back was to Barrow. He only grinned slightly.

'Far as I'm concerned, Babs,' he remarked, 'yore just as pretty from the back as from the front! And there aren't many gals y'can say that about!'

'You've done what you came to do, Poker,' Jeff snapped. 'Now get movin'. Remember what I told you about makin' cracks about Babs!'

Barrow shrugged. 'Okay. Just get this durned pipeline off my territory in double quick time, that's all . . . Let's go, sheriff.'

They returned to their waiting horses, mounted them, and rode away. Babs moved her head slowly as she watched them go, then she glanced at Jeff rather hopelessly as he stood thinking the matter out.

'It looks — as though he's won after all, Jeff, doesn't it?' she asked, sighing. 'I knew he'd think of something!'

'What's the matter? That big polecat got you mesmerised?' Jeff asked. 'He's pulled one out of the hat, sure — but that doesn't finish it.'

'I wish I could believe that,' the girl muttered.

'You can. I'll think of something when I've weighed up the situation. Let me see now . . . Only thing for it is to carry the pipeline round his territory. That's a tidy distance.'

He moved to low rock and squatted upon it, the girl beside him. She peered at the legal sheet in the glaring sunlight. For a long time Jeff studied it, looking at the terrain now and again as he did so.

'As I figger it,' he said finally, 'we're in the middle of the strip, which is just too bad. Had it been nearer one of the ends we could have just detoured. That means puttin' the top of the pipe diagonal instead of straight, and then addin' about three miles to the length — one an' a half to the right, a bend, and the one an' a half back again. Three miles,' he repeated, thinking. 'And working out at a thousand dollars a mile that's another three thousand.'

'We can pay it,' the girl said urgently. 'After that big win of yours at poker we're still about five thousand dollars in hand.'

'That's right . . . Yeh, we can afford it.'

There was something about the way Jeff spoke which made the girl look at him sharply.

'Then what's the matter?' she asked. 'The mining engineers will supply the pipes won't they? You sound as if you're worried about something.'

'I'm just wonderin' Babs . . . Poker knows I won eight thousand from him and he may also know that I should be able to pay for that extra piping — so I'm just asking myself what he's got at the back of his mind. At best his buyin' of this strip of land an' getting an injunction against me only amounts to delaying tactics. I figger there must be something deeper — but I don't know what it is.'

'Whether there's more behind it or not,' the girl said, 'we've just got to get that fresh piping ordered right away.'

'You said it,' Jeff got to his feet. 'Best thing I can do is have the men start dismantling — you can see that they do it properly — and then I'll take the train over to Stirling City this afternoon and see what I can fix up.'

5

It was towards sunset two nights later when a lone horseman rode up to the Lazy-T ranch and knocked urgently on the screen door. He was admitted by Barrow himself who motioned him into the living room.

'Well, Curly?' Barrow demanded, lighting the oil lamp. 'I've bin wonderin' how much longer you'd be getting here. How much did you find out?'

The puncher, dirt-plastered from a long ride, rubbed a hand over his tanned face.

'Purty near everythin', I reckon. They're sendin' them new pipes by railroad tomorrow night.'

'They are, huh?' Barrow's dark eyes glowed. 'By way of Paint Rock and Saba Mountain Cleft, I suppose?'

'That's right, boss. There just isn't no

other way inter this town.'

'Which is just as well,' Barrow commented, grinning. 'Okay, Curly, that's all I wanted to know. Get yourself some sleep; then stand by for fresh orders. Things are going to start happenin' around here mighty fast after tomorrow night.'

'They are?' the cowpuncher asked. 'What sort of things?'

'Never mind; you'll find out quick enough when I'm good an' ready. First I've a trip to make with about half a dozen of the boys. I reckon I ought to find most of 'em in the Twin Dollar at this time.'

The puncher nodded and went out with scuffling feet. Barrow stood musing for a moment or two, then he put a hand round the lamp chimney and blew out the flame. In a few minutes he was astride his horse, riding to the Twin Dollar. He grinned to himself as, in the twilight, working by kerosene flares to the accompaniment of the clangour of hammers, he could see the pipeline workers busy on their task of dismantling part of the pipe where it crossed his territory.

'An' tomorrow night, Mr Jeff Alroyd, you'll have a heap more to worry about,' he murmured. 'Try and play games with me, would you?'

He found the six cohorts he wanted at the tables in the Twin Dollar, and his plan began to take shape the following morning when, in the dawn light, he and his henchmen rode out of town to the south east.

Each of them was well watered and provisioned, prepared for a long and punishing ride which would bring them to the Saba Range and — if everything were correctly planned — to Saba Mountain Cleft itself by nightfall.

There were no slip-ups. Barrow had worked things out too carefully for that. At sunset he and his men gathered motionless on their horses, standing upon a broad plateau of rock which overlooked the railroad track a hundred feet below. The track emerged in two bright ribbons from a distant cleft in the rocks, passed below the promontory on which the men were waiting and then continued to the gradually flattening areas of the Texas prairies.

'Here she comes!' Barrow exclaimed at last, straightening up to sudden alertness. He stood motionless through a long interval, staring under his shading hand; then he nodded quickly. 'Okay, you know what to do, all of you. Let's be on our way.'

He swung round his horse's head and followed by his men — pulling their kerchiefs to their eyes as they went — they pursued a trail they had already selected down the rocky slope. Moving at top speed they came level with the track in about five minutes and they were still some three miles ahead of the slow-moving freight train.

'You, Jake, keep your eye on the horses,' Barrow ordered, jumping from his saddle. 'We'll be back . . . The rest of you come with me and keep down. If anybody happens to spot us the whole shoot's goin' to blow up in our faces.'

Using the myriad of rocks for shelter they dodged from one to the other, constantly coming nearer to the railroad track until they were only about three yards from the metals. Here they stopped and waited, still hidden, as the freighter came puffing and struggling up the incline, pulling its heavy load.

The hidden men waited until the engine was well past, then they sped forward, seized hold of the first convenient freight truck and swung up on to it. When they had mounted to its roof Barrow looked along the length of the train in the fast dying light.

'There — towards the back there!' Barrow exclaimed, pointing. 'That's the one we want. I can see the pipes from here — An' we've got to step on it!'

Leaping from truck to truck, hurrying along the giant logs of an extra long freighter wagon, they came finally to the medum-sized platform-wagon upon which was stacked a pyramid of metal pipes and, besides them, the unions with which they were to be later bolted together.

Standing with the train rocking him dangerously Barrow glanced about him. 'All right,' he breathed, his eyes gleaming. 'Just what we want! Get those chains unclamped, but don't quite release them. I'll tell you when. We want Saba Cleft, and that's another three mile or so further on — An' keep down!' he ordered. 'Get your blasted heads out of sight, can't you?'

He ducked and his men did likewise, moving carefully amidst the pipes until they had reached the chains holding them in position. The train squeaked and grated along the track, passing between high rock walls, up steep gradients, until at last it came within sight of the final promontory before the plains.

'Get ready,' Barrow instructed, his voice taut. 'Shouldn't be much further 'n here.'

His men nodded in the fading light but said nothing. At an increased speed the train progressed, reached the promontory, and then began to skirt it. To one side of the track was a vast gorge, all of four hundred feet in depth, its bottom lost in the gathered dark of night.

'Right,' Barrow snapped, and simultaneously he and his men jumped back with all the speed they could manage as the chains were released.

Fixedly they all watched the pipes rolling sideways from the wagon, impelled by the slight chasm-ward tilt of the track. They bounced and banged on to the rocks, went flying out into space and downwards, one after the other in a metallic clanging thunder which drowned even the grinding of the train wheels.

Barrow delivered a kick at the last remaining pipe, watched it roll out of position and keel over the side of the wagon; then he grinned behind his kerchief.

'Reckon that's that,' he said. 'Jeff Alroyd can come an' pick up the bits if he's so minded. Let's go — we're far enough from our horses as it is.'

He jumped down from the truck, stumbled, and fell amidst the rocks. One by one his cohorts followed him. For a while they stood watching the train continuing on its way, then they turned to retrace the journey to where Jake was waiting for them with the horses.

Advised by mail that a new consignment of pipeline would be at the railroad station the following morning for collection, Jeff and Babs set off there early — and once they arrived at the depot they received their first intimation of something having gone wrong.

'Y'mean to tell me,' Jeff snapped to the station master, after he had heard the man's gloomily told story, 'that those pipes just vamoosed between here an' Stirling City? That sort of thing isn't just possible! What kind of a yarn do you think you're telling?'

'I'm doing the best I can,' the station master replied impatiently. 'I'm on the phone now to Stirling City to find out what's happened. I've got the guard's manifest which sez them pipes wus on the train — truck 29 — last night when the train left Stirling. When the train drew in here that truck was empty. It sorta looks — far as we c'n tell at present — that the chains broke an' the pipes just naterally rolled off.'

'Then it's time somebody started lookin' for 'em!' Jeff retorted. 'I'll demand compensation from the railway for this! I'll be damned if I don't — '

'I reckon you can't do that,' the station master interrupted. 'They wasn't insured.'

Jeff tightened his lips and frowned.

'No, that's right,' Babs said, glancing at him anxiously. 'It would have cost more than we can afford to have insured them.'

'We must have been crazy,' he muttered. 'No matter how much it might have set us back we should have done that. We've just no way now of making a claim.'

'Jeff, what do you think is the explanation behind all this?'

'I c'n make a darned good guess,' he retorted; then glancing again at the station master. 'How long's it going to take to get some more news through?'

'Any time. There's men searchin' the track right now.'

As things transpired 'any time' proved to be early evening. All day long, barring the intervals when they broke for meals, Jeff and the girl were kept in a fever of anxiety at the station — then at last they received definite information.

'I reckon your pipes are lyin' smashed to bits in the bottom of Saba Cleft, jus' outside Paint Rock,' the station master announced. 'They've found 'em there. Only thing can be that as th' train swung round the bend in th' line the chains broke and — '

'Broke hell!' Jeff Alroyd interjected harshly. 'Unclamped more like it! All right, that's all I wanted to know.'

He caught Babs' arm and hurried her outside to the waiting buckboard.

'What now?' she demanded.

'Barrow!' he answered bitterly. 'Who else but that polecat could be behind all this? We've no claim on the railroad company since the stuff was at buyer's risk. Somehow Poker must have figgered things out beforehand and let those pipes smash to blazes at a point along the track. This is where him an' me are goin' to have words — an' if it comes to that it may not stop at words, either!'

He snapped the reins sharply on the team's withers and sent the buckboard careering down the main, twilight street of the ramshackle town. In the distance a lone cowpuncher perched on a roof and armed with a pair of field glasses — provided by Barrow — moved suddenly from his eyrie, vaulted down to the porch roof, and then hurried across the street.

He went straight to the Twin Dollar, flung open the batswings, and dived to the table where Barrow was seated playing cards.

'He's comin', boss,' he announced breathlessly. 'An' the dame's with him. From the lick he's movin' at I'd say he's good an' mad!'

'Okay.' Barrow seemed completely undisturbed. 'I figgered he'd come here to have it out with me. That's what the smart boys call psychology, see? All right, while he's here — an' the girl too, which makes it easier — that only leaves the old man and those labourers busy on that pipeline. Y'know what to do. Blast it to hell! Tear it out of the earth! Don't leave a single thing standing . . . Now blow!'

The men scattered and Barrow resumed his playing with his solitary partner. He slanted his eyes sideways as he saw the batwings suddenly open and shut; then Jeff came striding across the saloon with the girl close behind him. Barrow went on playing calmly.

'Just a minute, Poker!' Jeff's hands reached down and clamped about Barrow's wrist as he was about to lay down his cards. 'I want a word with you.'

Barrow looked up, his jaw set and his eyes hard. 'Okay. Start talkin'!'

'What's the idea of cowheeling my pipeline sections into the Saba Cleft?'

'The idea of what?' Barrow looked surprised; then he was suddenly whirled to his feet by main strength, Jeff's knotty fingers gripping the shoestring tie about his collar.

'So help me, Poker, I'm not jokin',' Jeff breathed, his eyes glinting. 'I know just what you did, an' if I can't get satisfaction any other way I can always take it out of your hide.'

'It would help a whole heap if I knew what yore talkin' about!' Barrow retorted, trying to pull free. 'What about your pipeline? Did you lose it some place? If so I reckon it ain't no more 'n you deserve.'

'You know damned well what's happened because you fixed it! Okay, now I aim to fix you — !'

Jeff's right hand suddenly dropped from Barrow's collar and drew back — but before he could aim the killing blow he had intended Barrow whipped up his chair and whirled it over his head. Just in time Jeff twisted sideways and instead of hitting his head it struck him across the back. He lurched and half fell across the table, dazed and gasping with nearly all the wind knocked out of him.

Instantly Barrow blurred his hands down to his guns, then gasped in anguish as Jeff back-kicked at him and took him in the stomach. The guns dropped out of his hands as he flattened his palms at his agonising middle. Jeff shook his head violently, twisted round, then lay on his back on the table, drawing up both knees to his chin.

With the force of uncoiling springs he jabbed his feet outwards and struck Barrow in the chest. Flung backwards by the impact he crashed into the next table and went down amidst it with beer glasses, cards, and table on top of him. Swearing cowpunchers went blundering out of his way. The women whirled their skirts and came to a halt at a safe distance, watching intently.

'Stop it!' Babs cried, running forward. 'Jeff! Poker! You'll never settle anything this way!'

'I reckon we can,' Jeff retorted, straightening up. 'It's the only kind of language this double-crossing jigger understands. Out of the way, Babs!'

'I won't!' she responded flatly. 'Our concern is the pipeline, not you two men beating each other up. I won't stand here and see you do it. Use commonsense, can't you?'

Poker lurched to his feet and grinned crookedly.

'He's right, angel,' he said grimly. 'We've been owin' each other a return match for some time — an' I'm achin' to take the nice new paint off him — Move, Babs!'

'I tell you I won't — '

The girl did not have the chance to finish. Jeff's hands seized her and she was tossed lightly to one side. Before he had hardly put her down Barrow's right landed straight in his jaw, snapping back his head. Jeff saw red: the vicious advantage taken of him destroyed his last scrap of reticence and he hit back savagely.

Out came his smashing left and Barrow went stumbling back into the 'orchestra'. He struggled up and a massive right-jab knocked him into a dizzy circle, forcing him to finally drop half across a table. In so doing his hand closed round a bottle. He smashed it quickly and swung round with the neck-end gripped in his fingers, the vicious, javelin-sharp points ready for a gouging movement.

Jeff dived, low down, missing the frightful weapon by inches. It struck the top of an overturned table and buried itself half an inch in the wood. Then Jeff's steel grip forced the bottle neck from Barrow's fingers. With his free hand Jeff rained punches into the gambler's upturned face; then he pulled him up and whipped round a hay-maker.

It took Barrow dead on the chin. He hurtled backwards, fell over the fallen bottles and a chair, and went smashing into the flimsy screen at the back of the orchestra. He essayed one effort to rise, then with blood streaked about his face he lay still and gasped heavily.

'I reckon that'll do — for the moment,' Jeff panted, rubbing his aching, sweating face. 'If there's any more to be said, Poker, I'm ready to say it in the same language — at any time. All right, Babs, it's time for us to get outa here.'

He caught her arm and, grim faced, strode through the wondering, interested gathering of punchers and saloon habitués. When they had reached the buckboard outside the girl looked at his bruised face in the kerosene lighting.

'I hope you're satisfied!' she exclaimed bitterly, a gleam of anger in her violet eyes.

'A bit,' he answered, then he gave her a questioning look as he started the horses moving. 'What's the matter,

Babs? Yore not the kind of gal who'd let a low down chiseller like that get away with it without answering back, are you?'

'Of course not — but what seems to escape you is the fact that while we wasted time there anything could have been happening to the pipeline! Back home I mean. It's dark now — and what didn't happen by day could happen by night. I wouldn't put anything past Poker.'

'Yeah . . . ' Jeff frowned to himself as he realised her woman's wit was a good deal sharper than his own. 'I never thought of that.'

'Don't I know it! All you saw was wading into Poker.'

'We've got to be movin'!'

Jeff urged the horses to greater speed, sweeping out of the town's high street in a whirl of dust and presently hitting the trail which led to the Double Circle and the valley two miles further on.

It was as the team raced on under the high-flung stars that there came across the silences the sound of firing. It was distinct and unmistakable even above the rattle of harness and grind of wagon wheels. Jeff suddenly felt the grip of the girl's hand and heard her anxious voice.

'Faster, Jeff!' she urged. 'That shooting can only be coming from our spread! It can't be at Poker's because he's at the Twin Dollar — and his ranch and ours are the only ones in this direction. I knew something was wrong,' she finished, in sudden tearful anxiety. 'I could feel it!'

Jeff whipped the team to even greater hurry along the remaining mile of trail, the wheels of the buckboard rattling in the dust and sun-baked soil, the girl and himself jolting up and down painfully on the hard wooden seat — Then as they rounded the last bend into the valley they came upon a sight which made the girl cry out and Jeff cracked his whip again over the furiously racing horses.

In the direction of the pipeline site timber was blazing and fire flared up into the night, carrying a pillar of burning sparks into the darkness. The mass of scaffold props which had been laid aside was burning savagely and at different points, like so many lighted candles, the supports of the existing pipe were being destroyed. Across the flame-shot darkness bullets were being exchanged, the noise of the explosions echoing in the confining walls of the valley.

The instant the buckboard and team came within range of the fracas Jeff dragged the snorting animals to a halt and jumped down, tugging out his .45s as he ran. Almost immediately he came upon one of his pipeline labourers as he crouched behind a rock, loading his revolver.

'What gives?' Jeff demanded, dropping beside him. 'Who's doin' all the shootin' around here?'

'Bandits, I reckon,' the man growled. 'They came down on us suddenly when darkness was settlin' — Howdy, miss,' he broke off, as Babs blundered into view and also crouched down in the fire-lighted gloom.

'Then what?' Jeff snapped.

'All we could do was scatter. We'd hardly time to draw our hardware. They had kerosene with them an' set fire to all th' wood. Some of the pipes they smashed with pickaxes — Wasn't as one-sided as it sounds, though. I guess we wounded some of them, too.'

Jeff set his mouth and peered over the rocks.

'Doesn't seem to be much firin' goin' on now,' he remarked.

'Nope. I reckon it's about over, Mr Alroyd. They done all they came to do — '

'Where's my father?' Babs interrupted suddenly.

'Last I seen on him, miss, he was over there, firin' with th' rest of 'em,' the man answered — and in sudden anxiety the girl scrambled to her feet and hurried in the direction the man indicated.

Jeff remained silent, watching, staring with bitter eyes at the kindling flames which were destroying everything he had so far built up — then he glanced round sharply at a sudden horrified cry from Babs. Immediately he jumped up and raced through the firelit gloom to where he found her on her knees beside a fallen figure.

'It's dad!' she cried hoarsely. 'He's — he's dead! I — I can't find any heartbeat — Oh, Jeff — !'

'Okay, take it easy,' he muttered, but his own examination only served to confirm the girl's grim suspicion. After a moment or two she realised what Jeff's silence meant and she began to weep convulsively.

'Can't be helped, kid,' Jeff murmured, putting an arm about her shoulders. 'I reckon he'd have wanted it this way — straight an' in the open air. Nothin' lingering.'

The girl did not answer but her shoulders shook.

'Call the sheriff,' Jeff ordered to the labourer who had come up. 'Get together what men there are and we'll be in the ranch-house when the sheriff starts his questioning. He'll want a full account of this night's work — and he'll get it. Have somebody bring in — the body. I'll look after Miss Kemp.'

'Okay, Mr Alroyd,' the man assented. 'Things should be safe enough now, I reckon. Those skunks have hit the trail from the look of things.'

His arms still about her shoulders Jeff led the girl into the ranch-house and lighted the lamps. She sank down into a chair and stared bleakly in front of her, tears still drowning her eyes.

'This is all Poker's doing,' she whispered. 'He murdered dad — '

'Though I hate Poker more 'n a bad smell, I don't think he'd be capable of doin' this,' Jeff said. 'We left him in the Twin Dollar, remember. Your dad got shot in the ordinary way of things — '

'Now you start defending Poker!' the girl shouted, leaping up, her cheeks flaming. 'Those outlaws were in his pay: that's what I mean! They shot dad and wrecked our pipeline — and all you do is start whitewashing Poker! If you think I'm going to stand for that — '

'All right, all right,' Jeff murmured, pushing her down in the chair again. 'Take it easy, Babs. Yore unstrung — an' I don't blame you. If you feel like cryin' — well, cry. It'll do you good.'

He turned aside and motioned the men to carry Morton Kemp's dead body into the adjoining bedroom and then shut the door. When this had been done he began a worried pacing of the living room whilst the labourers stood around in various positions, waiting. They glanced at one another uncomfortably, aware of the grim tension of tragedy in the atmosphere.

It seemed an age before Sheriff Hollows finally arrived, and by this time the girl was calmer, though her face was deathly pale and vindictively set.

'All right,' the sheriff said quietly, looking about him. 'Let me have the facts . . . An' let me have them slowly so's I can figger things out. What happened?'

The labourer whom Jeff had first contacted went through his story again with more detail and finished with a sudden burst of passion.

'If you ask me, sheriff, there ain't no two ways about it! That's what I say — an' the rest of us boys too! This is th' work o' that ornery cuss, Poker Barrow. Fust he bought up the land which meant a pipeline detour; then he wrecked th' new pipes on their way from Stirling City — Now he's burned everythin' up an' shot old man Kemp besides! I say he's ripe t'be the star turn at a necktie party.'

The assembly of men nodded grimly amongst themselves as the sheriff glanced at them.

'Best keep that sort of talk to yourself,' the sheriff said, his voice stern. 'There'll be no necktie parties whilst I'm around to administer the law. The law isn't concerned with how things look, remember — even though, as a man and one of the community, I'm inclined to agree with your views.'

He paused for a moment and paced about slowly thinking; then he resumed. 'Point is: there's nothin' can be proved. It certainly wasn't Barrow who shot Mr Kemp because he's been in the Twin Dollar all evening. I was there myself.'

Jeff glanced up. 'You were? In that case you must have seen him and me — ?'

'I saw you fightin', sure — but I didn't see any reason to interfere.' The sheriff gave a grim smile. 'The point I'm a-tryin' to make is this: We can't tie the murder of Mr Kemp on Barrow. It could ha' bin anybody. Anymore than we can prove that he gave the order to burn up the pipeline.'

'Then what are we supposed to do?' Babs demanded, getting up angrily. 'Does this mean that my father can be murdered and nobody is going to do anything about it? — just because of a lot of legal red tape. I'm not standing for that, sheriff, even if I have to go gunning for Poker myself! He's directly responsible for my father being killed

— or is it that you don't understand that?'

'I understand it, Miss Babs — mebby better'n any of you but unless yore plain crazy you won't go gunnin' for him. I'm takin' your father's body back to town and let Doc Ellison examine it an' take out the bullet — or bullets. It — or they — will be sent to Stirling City for examination by experts, an' a full report'll be sent back to me. Then we'll start lookin' for the gun that fired 'em. That's the legal procedure. When we have that we'll be a bit nearer.'

'When!' the girl echoed. 'The whole idea's ridiculous, and you know it! What's to stop the killer having thrown his gun away meantime?'

'Nothin' — only if he did that the fact that he's a gun short might be noticed . . . I don't think he'd care to risk that. That is the law as it has to be interpreted,' the sheriff added immovably, 'an' I'll have an inquest to hold. Can't do more than that right now — but I'm not sayin',' he finished significantly, 'that you can't try and dig up some proof for yourselves, providin' you stay on the right side of the law.'

Nobody spoke. They all stood watching in silence as one of the labourers gave the sheriff a hand to carry the dead Kemp's body out of the ranch-house, then the girl sank back in her chair again and buried her face in her hands.

'You fellers get back to the bunk-house,' Jeff ordered. 'I'll join you later on. Reckon I'll doss with you now the old man's dead . . . In th' daylight we'll see what damage was done, an' if there's anythin' can be saved.'

The men nodded and went out quietly, closing the main door. Jeff stood in silence, looking down at the girl.

'I think,' she said at last, glancing up and fighting for control, 'that I'm — I'm calming down a bit now . . . He's gone, and it'll take me an awful time to get used to it. As for us — it looks as if we're finished. No more float money left, the pipeline smashed up, and that hyena Poker laughing his ugly head off!'

'We've had a licking, and a big one — 'specially as far as yore concerned,' Jeff said quietly, putting a gentle hand on the girl's arm. 'But we're not going to let Barrow win that easily. Only thing for it is to start again — with a deck of cards.'

Babs gave a hopeless shrug.

'You mean you're going to try and get money again by gambling? That it?' She sighed. 'Oh, what's the use, Jeff? Now dad's gone I don't care what happens to this confounded ranch. It's caused more than enough trouble and tragedy already. I hate the place, and everything, connected with it.'

'Including me?'

'No — not you, Jeff,' she said seriously. 'I'll never feel that way about you. But outside that everything does look pretty bleak.'

'It won't — in time,' he assured her, with an encouraging smile. 'Take my word for it. I'm outside your grief an' I can think straighter. We're going on — or at anyrate I am. An' so will you when you've recovered from this knock. To crawl away and just leave Barrow to his victory isn't your line of action, I reckon.'

The girl said nothing for a moment, then her chin tightened a little.

'No,' she admitted, 'it isn't. Dad wouldn't have thought much of me, either, if I'd crawled away under a rock. Just let me get over this shock, then I'll see things in better perspective.'

6

The following morning, after he had spent the night — for the sake of ethics — with the men in the bunkhouse, Jeff found the girl almost normal again, even though she admitted that she had spent a sleepless night.

'I'm with you, Jeff,' she said, when they were at breakfast. 'Dad would have wanted it this way — and I'm fortunate in having you to handle things.'

'That's more like it,' he murmured. 'I've been reckoning up money too. There's about five hundred dollars left in the bank, isn't there?'

'Six-fifty, to be exact, and I'm quite willing to leave it to you to decide what to do with it.'

'Five hundred 'll do. Durin' the morning you'd better draw it out. You can get the necessary authority from lawyer Billings now your dad is dead.

With that five hundred I've got to win enough to buy a pipeline all over again.'

'You will.' Babs said, with quiet assurance. 'I don't forget the last time. With the way you can play a deck you can get away with it again.'

'And after breakfast,' Jeff added, 'we've the unpleasant job of lookin' over last night's dirty work.'

They both found that 'unpleasant' had been an understatement in that there was not a single part of the pipeline left in one piece. The bone-dry timber piles had been burned to grey ashes; every pipe was fractured by repeated blows from picks. There was just nothing that could be done. The labourers looked about them gloomily as they accompanied Jeff and the girl on their harrowing tour of inspection. In the end they felt as though they had been round a scrap-heap.

'Yeah, he sure made a thorough job of it whilst he was about it,' Jeff admitted finally. 'Okay, Babs, it's time we got into town and to the bank.'

He took her arm and they returned to the ranch for the buckboard and team. Scarcely speaking to each other, so sombre were their thoughts, Jeff drove into town and they had completed their business with lawyer Billings and the bank by the time mid-morning had arrived.

Jeff was just in the act of buttoning the five hundred dollars into his shirt pocket before whipping up the horses for the return trip home when Sheriff Hollows came into view along the boardwalk.

'Hello there, sheriff, how far have you got?' the girl called, and at the sound of her voice he glanced in her direction and came forward, touching his hat.

'Mornin', Miss Babs — Mr Alroyd,' he acknowledged, and his eyes travelled briefly over the sombre black dress the girl was wearing. 'I've only got the news that two bullets killed your father — but I reckon you won't want to hear about those sort of facts.'

'I more than want to,' the girl told

him. 'I insist on it! Tell me everything there is to know, sheriff. I've gotten over the shock by now.'

'Okay then,' Hollows assented, shrugging. 'It was a coupla forty-fives which finished him — one in th' heart and another in the stomach. The fact that they're forty-fives might well help us, too. They're a bit rare around here. One more usually finds thirty-eights. On top of the bullets are queer striker-pin marks, so once the gun that fired 'em is found there won't be much trouble in gettin' identification . . . Right now the bullets are on their way by insured mail to Stirling City. I'm holding an inquest this afternoon just to range up a few facts. I was comin' over to tell you but meetin' you'll save me the trouble. You must both attend. I'll adjourn the verdict of the inquest, until I've gotten some more facts — but you'll be able to bury your father decent, Miss Babs.'

'Thanks, sheriff,' she said quietly. Then after a long pause during which she thought over what he had said she added: 'Very well, Mr Hollows — we'll be at the inquest.'

With a nod the sheriff went on his way and Jeff whipped the team into action. He and the girl had been seated in silence and were half way through the leisurely journey home when she spoke, slowly and haltingly, as though she had to force the words out.

'I've just noticed something about you, Jeff, which I suppose I should have noticed before. You wear forty-fives!'

He glanced down at his guns. 'Yeah, sure I do.' Then as she remained silent he stared at her. 'For Pete's sake, Babs, yore not tyin' up those slugs found in your dad's body with these rods of mine, are you?'

'No, no, of course not!' And he knew from her tone and the look in her violet eyes that she meant what she said. 'But I'm just thinking — There'll be plenty who'll know you wear forty-fives, especially those who work for Poker, and they may try to pull something. Anyway I can't see them passing up the chance to perhaps cash in on the coincidence.'

Jeff shrugged. 'Okay, let 'em. All guns fire differently, remember. Mine, on examination, would obviously be proven innocent of firing those murder bullets.'

'I'm sure of that, Jeff, but . . . ' The girl reflected and then sighed. 'Yes, I suppose that's right. Only it's an uneasy coincidence which I don't like. Poker's such a deep card . . . Jeff, please don't think I ever suspected you of anything. I know you couldn't have: I was with you all the time until I — I found dad.'

Jeff smiled and gently urged the horses onwards.

⋆   ⋆   ⋆

Poker Barrow sprawled at his ease in the living room of his ranch-house, a glass of whisky on the table beside him, a cheroot in his mouth. His eyes narrowed in the strong fumes as he contemplated the henchmen who had just arrived.

'All right, Curly,' he said, 'let's have it.'

'Jeff Alroyd and the Kemp dame went to the lawyer's after lookin' over th' mess of last night,' Curly said, grinning momentarily, 'and then they went to th' bank. After that they had a word with the sheriff — but it weren't intentional. He wuz just passin'. I've no notion as to what he told 'em. Couldn't risk lettin' meself be seen, of course. Then they rode back home. I reckon they're there right now ... Which seems to cover everythin'.'

Barrow removed his cheroot from his teeth, took a drink, and became thoughtful.

'I expect they'll have an inquest to attend today — seein' that they found the old man's body,' he commented. 'I shan't be called 'cos I'm not supposed to be mixed up in it! An' it was Jake who got the old man?'

'He sure did — jest like you ordered. All th' same, I can't quite figger your angle, boss.'

'It's simple enough,' Barrow replied calmly. 'My reasonin' is that with her old man dry-gulched and th' pipeline wiped out that gal will quit — leave the district, and where she goes that smart guy Alroyd 'll go too. That way we get rid of 'em . . . But bein' the man I am I've an alternative plan in case they stop, and now it looks as if they mean to. In fact I'd say it's plumb certain.'

'I don't see how you c'n be sure of it.'

'Simply by th' fact that they aren't showin' any signs of leavin' the spread, or dismissin' those pipeline labourers — and also by th' fact that they've been to th' bank. How much money they have left I don't know, but I don't think it'll measure up to buyin' another lot of pipeline. So there's only one way they can do it — or Alroyd can — and I'll bet that it's by another card gamble.'

'Playin' you, you mean?'

'He will if he has the chance; I'm sure of that.' Barrow gave a faint grin. 'If he does — which is what I expect — my alternative plan goes into action.'

135

'Am I supposed to know what it is?' the puncher asked.

'You sure are. Jeff Alroyd wears forty-fives, which is one reason why I had Jake use a forty-five to blot out old man Kemp.'

Barrow opened a drawer in the table beside him and put his hand inside it. He withdrew it again with his first finger in the barrel of a .45.

'This is the gun,' he explained, with a grim smile. 'All prints on it have been wiped off, and there's no reason why I should put any on. Tonight, if — as I believe — Alroyd starts playin' poker, this gun has got to be slipped into one of his holsters an' his own forty-five removed. An' there haven't got to be any fumblings or mistakes about the way it's done, either.'

'Without leavin' prints on that gun?' Curly asked doubtfully. 'I reckon that won't be too easy.'

Barrow looked irritated. 'S'pose you use that block o' wood on your shoulders to do a bit of thinkin' now an' again?' he suggested. 'Plenty o' punchers wear gloves. You'll do just that — an' you'll make yourself look respectable to match 'em! Try shavin' for a change!'

'So you want me to slip him that hardware?'

'Yeah. He doesn't know you. Once you've slipped it to him leave the rest to me. I'm goin' to be sure the sheriff's around too.'

'Okay.' Curly manoeuvred the gun to the end of his finger and then pushed it inside his shirt. 'An' you'd better hold his attention good an' hard, boss, else I'll never be able to make it.'

'Y'can trust me to do that. There's nobody he'd sooner soak than me so he'll play with all the attention he's got when he finds I'm ready. An' that'll be your chance to get things movin'.'

Curly reflected. 'An' s'pose he takes you for a hayride as he did last time?'

An ugly look crossed Barrow's handsome face. 'Ain't no partic'lar reason to remind me about that, is there?' he snapped.

'Just a thought,' the puncher explained, shrugging.

'He'll take me for no rides this time,' Barrow declared flatly. 'Because you'll be standin' right behind him an' you'll use those signals we've agreed on. I'll outplay him at every turn and with a straight deck which he c'n examine with a microscope if he wants. I'll fix that jigger this time, believe you me . . . Okay you can blow.'

Curly nodded and took his departure. With a smile Barrow picked up his whisky glass and drained it.

'Yes, Mr Alroyd, you'll have one helluva job tryin' to work your way outa this one,' he mused. 'Sheriffs don't dare give murderers the breaks, I reckon . . .'

★ ★ ★

It was seven-thirty when Jeff entered the Twin Dollar, and with him was Babs. In vain he had argued that she should stay at the ranch, that the girl's very anxiety might be unconsciously conveyed to him and put him off his stroke — but she would have none of it. With her own future at stake as well as his she was determined to be present.

The gaming saloon was as busy as ever, with its rank atmosphere, noise, and diverse scattering of men and women. Jeff's eyes went slowly over the assembly and paused at length on two figures at a distant table. He smiled to himself and nudged the girl.

'Barrow,' he murmured. 'Looks like the luck's with us, Babs. This is just what I was hopin' for.'

'Nothing unusual about him being here,' Babs answered. 'He's here every evening — But look, Jeff,' she went on anxiously, 'why do you have to play him?'

'Why? Listen to the gal! Because it's the nateral thing to do, of course.'

'Yes, but you know he only gambles and wins because he plays crooked: and we can't afford risks like that. The hazard's high enough as it is. There are plenty of other poker players — Denham, over there in the corner, for instance. He's a pile of money and plays straight — '

'I'm playin' Barrow,' Jeff broke in obstinately. 'It's one of the few joys of my life to take that loudmouthed chiseller for everything he's got. Come on!'

With a sigh the girl followed him reluctantly across the big room. Out of the tail of his eye Barrow saw the two approaching and glanced up. He grinned widely.

'What's the matter?' he enquired dryly. 'Spoilin' for another fight?'

'Mebby,' Jeff answered, looking down on him steadily. 'I know plenty, Poker, but I can't prove it.'

'You seem to spend all your time in that sort of spot, Alroyd. An' it sort of makes it waste of time you talkin', doesn't it? If yore not here to fight, what do you want?'

'A game — if yore not too leary.'

'Leary?' Poker shrugged. 'Reckon I

can match you. Blow, you,' he added to Curly, and the neatly dressed, begloved cowpuncher threw in his cards and got up.

Jeff slid into the vacant chair, unbuttoned his shirt pocket and threw down a sealed deck of cards.

'My own this time,' he explained grimly. 'Or rather the late Morton Kemp's. In case you're not wise to the fact he got drilled last night.'

'I know,' Poker responded coolly. 'I was at the inquest this afternoon, sittin' in the audience listenin' to your fancy speeches . . . Too bad he got himself bush-whacked. Just the way of the west, I s'pose.'

'So that's what you call it?' Jeff asked.

'Sure do. Any other angles?'

Jeff studied the gambler fixedly for a moment with his cold grey eyes, then he glanced up at the girl by his side. She was not alone, either. A gathering of men and women, Curly in the forefront and just behind Jeff's left shoulder had assembled to watch this second card battle of the giants, most of them hoping it would be every bit as exciting as its predecessor.

'Fetch the sheriff, Babs,' Jeff ordered.

Barrow's complacent grin faded a little as though he wondered what was coming. He disguised his feelings by lighting a cheroot — and presently Sheriff Hollows appeared.

'Somebody want me?' he enquired, and Jeff handed him the deck of cards.

'Open these, sheriff, and check 'em,' he invited. 'Just to be sure there's no funny business — on my part anyway.'

The Sheriff gave a grim smile as he tore the wrapper.

'You two trust each other like a coupla prairie dogs, don't you?' He went through the cards skilfully and put them down again. 'They're clean,' he announced.

The ante was staked at two hundred and Jeff dealt the cards. He won the first hand and apparently without any great effort. The game went on again with the silent watchers following every move intently.

Curly shifted position and rubbed the end of his sawn-off nose. Because of his action Jeff lost the next pot, but as far as he could detect from a brief glance around him, there was no trickery going on. He and Barrow were even again on the ante.

For ten minutes the two men played back and forth with increasing tenseness. Curly glancing slyly about him, satisfied that every eye was on the game ... Long and adept in surreptitious movement he presently withdrew the .45 revolver from his own holster and held it straight down at his side in his gloved hand. Thus he remained for a moment or two, then under the pretext of stooping to pick up his fallen cigarette he switched the gun from Jeff's left-hip holster, which was projecting temptingly over the edge of the chair.

Barrow, his face immovable, went on playing. 'See yuh,' he said, moving a pile of chips.

'A flush,' Jeff said exposing his cards.

'A full,' Barrow countered, and

scooped the pool again. Jeff's brow darkened and he looked puzzled. He glanced up into the anxious face of Babs. His supply of chips was running low.

'What's this game for, anyway?' Barrow asked presently. 'Is it just to amuse yourself, or is it so's you can buy up some more pipeline?'

'Pipeline,' Jeff retorted. 'An' since you destroyed all the other pipeline I'm goin' to make you pay for it — the hard way!'

'You are huh? Well, yore not doin' so good up t' now . . . ' Barrow slapped down his cards emphatically on the table. 'In fact,' he decided, getting up, 'I don't think I'm playin' on any further. I'm no saint, I reckon — everybody knows it — but I don't like sittin' playin' with a murderer!'

Jeff jumped up from his chair and seized Barrow fiecely across the table.

'What in thunder d'you mean by that?' he demanded. 'Never mind wrapping it up with a fancy approach.'

'It's plain enough,' Barrow answered, with a sneering smile. 'Everybody here knows from th' inquest that old man Kemp died from a forty-five slug — an' I've just happened to notice that you wear forty-fives yourself! I never bothered to look before, though I guess I should've — '

'These?' Jeff yanked out his guns; then he gave a start as he looked at the left-hand weapon. 'What's the — ?' he breathed, gazing about him in mystification. 'There's something mighty screwy goin' on around here — '

'What's the matter?' Barrow asked dryly. 'Scared of your own rods?'

'Somebody's frisked my gun and handed me this,' Jeff snapped, brandishing it in the air. 'Who the — '

'Yore not makin' a very good job of keepin' your mouth shut, are you?' Barrow asked. 'Sheriff, mebby you'd better take a look at this gun of Alroyd's. Seems to me you might find it interestin'.'

Sheriff Hollows, at the rear of the

assembly, pushed his way forward. He looked at Jeff's bemused expression and then held out his hands. Slowly Jeff handed the guns over. The sheriff snapped open the left-hand .45 and glanced at it.

'Two bullets missing,' he announced. 'Just a moment, folks — stand back.'

When a clearance had been made he fired once into the woodwork of the wall and then went over with his open pen-knife to dig out the bullet. The crowd, Jeff, Barrow and Babs in the forefront, crushed round him. He held up the bullet between finger and thumb for all to see.

'I reckon there isn't much doubt about it,' he said quietly. 'The striker-pin mark on this bullet is the same as those on the ones which killed Mr Kemp — or leastways it looks to be, with the naked eye. I'll get experts to check on it as quick as they can.'

'This is absurd!' Babs declared angrily. 'You heard Jeff say this gun had been switched. That isn't his gun — I know that myself!'

'Fact remains, Miss Babs, that it was in his holster and it's the gun I'm lookin' for,' Hollows responded. 'Sorry but that's the way it is. You'd best come along with me, Alroyd, whilst I get things checked up.'

'To — to jail?' Jeff gasped blankly. 'But dammit, I — '

'Sorry. You know the law as well as I do. If this gun isn't yours it'll be proven finally. Until then yore under arrest on suspicion. I reckon yore not the kind of chap to start makin' things tough for me . . . and yourself.'

Jeff looked about him helplessly, hesitating over making a sudden dash for it; then he saw that the sheriff had his own gun levelled.

'Shouldn't try anythin', Alroyd, if I was you,' he warned. 'Let's go quietly.'

7

There was no sleep for Babs Kemp that night. Immediately after Jeff had been taken by the sheriff she had left the Twin Dollar and ridden back in the buckboard to the ranch. In the silence of the living room — and later wakeful in bed — she went over the situation from every angle. And the more she thought about it the blacker the picture seemed to become, and the lower her spirits sank.

How the gun had got into Jeff's holster did not concern the law. It would only be interested in the fact that it was in his possession and that it was the one which had killed Morton Kemp, for Babs had no illusions but what the expert would prove it to be the one.

The only other way of escape — that of proving an alibi — was likewise washed out since at the approximate time of the murder she and Jeff had been on their way home to the ranch, with nobody but themselves to corroborate the fact. Her word alone would not be accepted without verifying evidence from other witnesses — and there were none.

Finally, unless some very conclusive proof could be found to show that Barrow was at the back of everything, it was even possible that the law might order that Jeff Alroyd must die, a victim of circumstantial evidence. This was a thought which was instantly terrifying in its possibility.

'There's got to be a way!' Babs breathed desperately to herself. 'There's got to be!'

But as far as she could see there was not. Appealing to Poker would be worse than useless, she realised. He had deliberately set himself out to destroy Jeff and the pipeline project — and even perhaps had a vague hope of winning her back again into the bargain. That he would ever confess to having murdered her father was wishing for the moon indeed. On the other hand his own men would never betray him for fear of how such action might rebound on them.

By dawn Babs had not slept. Wearily she clambered out of bed, dressed herself, and wandered into the living room to gather together a breakfast she did not really want. She ate it perfunctorily and had just finished it and was contemplating asking the advice of the pipeline labourers in her dilemma when there was an authoritative pounding on the screen-door. Puzzled, she got up and walked swiftly into the hall. She got a surprise upon opening the screen-door and beholding Poker Barrow's tall, rangy form standing there, his horse tethered to the rail of the porch.

'Howdy, Babs,' he greeted, and pushed his way in as he pulled off his hat. 'Surprised, huh?'

'You're just about as welcome as a

snake,' she retorted, holding the door wide. 'Get out, before I have the boys throw you out!'

Barrow grinned impudently and half perched himself on the edge of the table.

'Mebby you'd better hear what I have to say first — that is if your bright new boyfriend is your main anxiety.'

Babs closed the door slowly and came over to him, hope struggling with the anger in her expression.

'You mean you're going to help him?' she asked blankly. 'Is that it?'

'I sure am — bein' of a generous disposition. But of course there's a price.'

'Naturally! I would hardly have expected anything else from a man like you!'

'It's all perfectly simple,' Barrow said, spreading his hands. 'You sign this entire ranch over to me — and the land of course — an' your boyfriend goes as free as the air.'

'By admitting that you murdered my

father, I suppose?' the girl asked cynically.

'I didn't murder him.' Barrow's expression was perfectly bland. 'But I know who did — an' so will the sheriff the moment the property is mine . . . ' He glanced about him. 'I can make good use of it, Babs, dividin' the water course. I c'n double my income and mebby treble it. You an' your boyfriend can blow town, a murderer will get what he deserves, an' everybody lives happily ever after. In fact everythin' workin' out just the same as it does in the story books.'

'You mean,' Babs said slowly, 'that you intend to get this ranch and land for nothing in return for the murderer of my father being handed over.'

'Y'don't have to be so blunt about it do you?'

'Is it the truth or isn't it?' the girl demanded. 'I'm in no mood for playing around with the issue, Poker!'

'Okay,' he agreed shrugging. 'That's the setup, yes — an' I'll gamble you'll agree because Alroyd's freedom means more to you than this wreck you've gotten yourself saddled with.'

Babs gave a contemptuous smile. 'And you've no qualms whatever about giving away one of your own men?'

'None at all. He's a killer anyway — so he'll only get what he deserves. I know of three murders he's committed right in this district — barrin' the murder of your father.' Barrow stood up straight, his bantering tone toughening. 'That's the stake, Babs,' he said curtly. 'What's the answer?'

For a long time the girl was silent then she said briefly:

'I've got to have time to think it out, Poker. Give me until this hour tomorrow.'

'Right,' he assented. 'But if you've any sense at all you'll see that you've no alternative . . . I'll be right here after breakfast in the mornin'.'

He turned and departed, leaving the girl in thought. The dim beginnings of an idea were at the back of her mind.

As the morning advanced they took clearer shape — to the extent of leading her to experiment with the pack of cards with which Jeff had shown her one or two neat and effective tricks. She found upon further practice that she had certainly not lost her touch.

In the afternoon she attended the simple funeral of her father at the town chapel, and though she would have liked to have lingered longer at the grave to pay her last farewell, her plans urged her onwards. She went to the offices of the local newspaper and there remained for an hour.

By the evening her scheme was fully matured, and the habitues of the Twin Dollar were surprised at the sight of her entering the saloon alone so soon after her father had been laid to rest. One or two punchers winked at each other as they noticed that a gun-belt with a .38 packed in the holster was slapping against the right side of her riding skirt.

Her face grim she pushed her way through the mob of men and women and finished her course at Barrow's table. As usual he was playing poker, and there was no acting about the surprise on his face. He was genuinely staggered.

'What gives?' he asked blankly, as the girl's violet eyes fixed on him.

'Nothing to stop me playing a game of poker, is there?' she asked him briefly. 'And if you don't mind, I think I'll play with you.'

'For what?' Barrow asked. 'Or have you forgotten that your boyfriend was cleaned out last night before the sheriff took him away?'

'I've fifty dollars here,' the girl responded, 'and I'm playing it — win or lose. Thanks to your low-down thieving I can't make the ante any higher.'

Barrow frowned, motioned the men with whom he had been playing to quit the table, and then the girl seated herself. She glanced about her, caught sight of Sheriff Hollows hovering in the background. He caught her look and came forward.

'Howdy, Miss Kemp,' he greeted. 'Bit unusual to see you sittin' here. Anythin' I can do?'

'You can stay right here, sheriff, just to see that I'm not gypped by this vulture,' and Babs gave a cold stare at Barrow's suspicious face across the table.

She put down her chips to the value of $30 and Barrow did likewise. Then the game began, watched as usual by the circle of interested men and women. Curly stood right behind the girl but she stooped so closely over her cards he could not even glimpse what they were. To Barrow's profound annoyance there were no warning signals and he was compelled to play straight. In consequence, because it was so long since he had done so, he felt almost foreign to the game.

He felt a little happier at winning the first hand, but thereafter he definitely began to lose. The ante rose from 30 dollars to 50 dollars and again the girl cleaned it out. It went up to 800 dollars, and then 1,000 dollars, and again she won on a straight flush. Barrow sat staring at her fixedly, a darker colour in his complexion.

'What is this?' he snapped. 'Who taught you to play poker like yore doin'?'

'Never mind,' she answered him levelly. 'I'm staking my ranch and this thousand dollars against ten thousand dollars of yours, Poker.'

'You are, huh? An' s'posin' I don't like the stake?'

'Leary?' the girl asked contemptuously, and Barrow's eyes glinted.

'Ten thousand it is!' he snapped, and pushed the chips into position.

The girl dealt the cards and there was a long, ominous silence as they both considered their hands. Both players discarded and drew two cards.

'Triplets,' Barrow announced, putting his cards on view on the table. 'I win!'

'You lose, Poker.' Babs laid her own cards in front of her. 'A straight!'

'There's somethin' crooked goin' on

here!' Barrow exploded, jumping up. 'I'm not payin' ten thousand for this! It's not even nateral for a gal to — '

'Yore payin', feller,' Sheriff Hollows interrupted. 'This game's bin on the level. I've been watchin' it. You got yourself beaten by a better player, that's all. Mebby it stings to be beaten by a woman, but it's the truth, whether you like it or not.'

'Maybe he lost because he hadn't anybody to make signs over his shoulder,' the girl suggested coldly. 'There was a lot of that business went on last night; I saw it. It didn't dawn on me at the time what it meant; but it did during the day. You're no poker player, Poker! You're a two-bit swindler — '

'What in the heck do you want all this money for?' Barrow raved. 'You can't build a pipeline without Alroyd! He's the brain of the outfit and — '

'You mean you didn't know?' Babs asked in surprise. 'He's comin' out of jail tomorrow — proven innocent. Jake confessed.'

'Jake — confessed? He can't have!' Barrow cried. 'That is, unless you made him — '

He broke off, looking into the muzzle of the girl's .38 as she pointed it at him steadily. There was a deadly silence, and profound puzzlement crossed Sheriff Hollows' face.

'Sheriff — ' Babs glanced at him briefly. 'Would you call that a confession of the fact that Jake murdered my father, or not?'

'I sure would,' Hollows snapped. 'I — No you don't!' he broke off, as a cowpuncher made to break through the circle. 'Stand right where you are! Take it easy, Jake — I've got you covered.'

Jake hesitated and then became motionless. He glared across at Barrow vindictively.

'Okay — but he made me do it!' he snapped. 'I'm not a-takin' the rap fer it — an' I don't know how this dame found out either. Yore a dirty stool pigeon, Poker — '

'I never told her anythin'!' Barrow

shouted. 'Keep your damned mouth shut!'

'All I did was use my brains,' the girl explained calmly. 'The guy who committed the murder had already committed three murders in this district. I spent the afternoon in the newspaper offices looking through the files. I found a report of all the shootings and editorials about them too. Those editorials did everything but call Jake by his name. Description and everything else fitted exactly. I knew who it was ... so I tricked you into making a confession. Simple as that. See?'

'You — hellcat!' Barrow breathed, his colour dark. 'I'll durned well — '

'You'll pay me ten thousand dollars in cash right now,' Babs stated. 'And I shan't leave here until you do. And you, sheriff, have got the man you want. You'll find that the guns were switched last night, as Jeff said.'

'Sure they were,' Jake agreed. 'Curly there did it. I tell yuh that Barrow's the man y'want, sheriff.'

'I'll be the best judge of that,' Hollows retorted. 'I only want you at the moment. You've opened your mouth wide enough to choke yourself this time, Jake. Go on — start movin'!'

'Before you go,' the girl said, catching Hollows' arm. 'Would you mind seeing to it that Poker pays me what he owes? It's more than likely he may try and get out of it. I can't be as persuasive as a man, remember.'

Hollows nodded and gave the gambler a grim look.

'I reckon you'd best get it, Barrow. I don't care how. The girl won it in a straight game an' she's entitled. I'm not moving 'til she gets what's due her.'

Barrow set his mouth and then jerked his head to the distant saloon owner. He came hurrying over quickly . . .

Released from jail that night Jeff heard the whole story of the girl's unusual strategy to get at the truth. When she had finished he laughed heartily because he could not help himself.

'Durn me!' he ejaculated, as he and the girl sat in the ranch-house living room, 'I reckon it takes a woman to settle things! All we men think of is a gun or a fist — but you used your noodle, an' how you used it! Ten thousand dollars an' a confession squeezed out of Barrow! In fact the only thing wrong in the whole setup is that he'll stay free. Can't prove anythin' against him, I'm afraid. Jake's word alone won't do.'

'That doesn't matter,' the girl said, brushing the issue aside. 'Jake will pay the penalty, and that's as it should be since he fired the gun. My main object was to find the real murderer of my father, and now I've done it I'm satisfied. Poker's own double-dealing will catch up with him finally; that's inevitable. In the meantime we start the pipeline again, I suppose?'

'You bet we do!' Jeff declared. 'First thing tomorrow we're goin' to Stirling City to fix up another consignment for that pipeline of ours — '

'We?'

'That's what I said. You don't think I'm leaving you here when Barrow might take a crack at you for what you've done, do you? He'll be rank poison from now on ... Yeah,' Jeff mused, 'we'll order fresh stuff, double the labour force — now we've a good deal of money — and have men watching the pipes as the train brings 'em. The result should be that we'll really finish the job at last. We'll not give Barrow another chance no matter what we do.'

Nor did they. With a redoubled labour force, a constant watch night and day, and every man heavily armed — and at night the girl sleeping with armed watchmen guarding the ranch's exterior — even Poker Barrow realised that for the moment he was beaten in his efforts to prevent the building of the pipeline — but that did not prevent him from turning schemes over in his mind.

He was forced to watch the pipeline growing longer, bending at right angles when it reached his own pegged-out territory snaking round it, and then continuing diagonally across the valley. Finally it appeared to him that there was only one course left open to him.

Three of his henchmen — there had been four until Jake had paid the price for his murdering activities — only knew what the plan was when, three weeks later, just after dawn, Barrow led them on a climb into the Apache Mountains, pausing finally at a high eminence where, far below on a gently grading slope, the pipeline was visible, and the men assembling in readiness for the day's work.

'Look at 'em,' Barrow murmured, leaning on the saddle horn and gazing down. 'Like flies round a honeypot . . . An' this scheme's so plumb easy I don't know why we didn't think of it at first. No blame attachin', no anythin'. Just what you might call a nateral catastrophe!'

The three men with him glanced up and down the narrow mountain trail in puzzlement, then at each other. Barrow caught their baffled looks and grinned.

'The answer's right in front of you,' he said calmly. 'You see those balanced rocks at the side of th' trail? What happens if any one of 'em shifts?'

The punchers thought it out.

'I reckon half the mountan side 'd come down with the under-pinnings pushed away,' Curly answered finally. 'Same as happened before when that stream got diverted to your pastures — '

'Right! An' the rocks'll go straight down — an' if it wipes out that pipe and the party below, what happens? Act of God! Who's to prove the rocks were pushed? If somebody gets hurt in the process, as they probably will, I reckon we can't help that, can we?'

The men looked at each other again and then smiled and nodded. They slid from their horses as Barrow dismounted and crossed to the nearest upended spire. Barrow examined it for a while and then turned.

'Okay, we shove,' he announced.

'Then we get back quick. Once it's gone all these other rocks round it 'll start to get on the move too . . . Let's get started.'

Gently he applied pressure and then increased it. His three colleagues added their own strength. By degrees the big balanced rock began to sway gently back and forth — then suddenly it went over the plumbline of the perpendicular and rolled heavily away from them, bouncing and leaping into the air, sweeping down the sloping mountain side and carrying with it a mass of smaller boulders.

These in turn dislodged the supports of the massive rocks nearby and they too shivered and shifted and began rolling. An ever increasing avalanche began to thunder downwards towards the party working on the pipe far below, gathering noise and speed as it travelled.

What happened Barrow and his men could not see since a haze of dust which arose blotted out everything. When at last it had settled they beheld one half of the pipeline buried and the scattered figures did not seem as numerous. They were milling about quickly on various urgent errands. Some were digging in the rocks.

'Not so good,' Barrow muttered disappointedly, tugging out field-glasses and taking care to remain well hidden as he focussed them. 'The main rock mass went one-sided and only wiped out half the pipe instead of all of it. Alroyd's still there — Yeah, an' the girl too! I can see 'em! I thought we'd got 'em — Hell!' he finished in alarm.

His men waited, suddenly tense at his change of tone. After a long, steady scrutiny he lowered his glasses and gazed at his cohorts somewhat dazedly.

'I'll be damned,' he breathed. 'The avalanche has blocked the stream to my pastures!'

'What!' Curly ejaculated, starting.

'It's not flowing into the valley at all now,' Barrow went on savagely. 'Completely blocked up. No sign of it. Babs Kemp and Alroyd aren't getting the benefit, but neither am I! An' from the look of that rock pile down there, there ain't much hope of puttin' things straight, either.'

'It looks,' Curly said, rubbing his whiskery chin, 'as if your 'Act of God' has misfired a bit, boss. Freein' that stream jus' can't be done with Alroyd on the scene of operations. He'll stop you, even if it's with bullets. You've given him the hell of a job straightening out his pipe — but yore goin' to have a bigger one to get any water at all. I reckon you thought up one scheme which skidded you from the word 'Go'.'

'Yeah . . . ' Barrow gazed pensively into distances. 'Yeah, I reckon yore right. I've got to do some fast thinkin' — an' I've got to do it quick.'

★　★　★

After sunset that evening, when they had just finished their supper, Jeff and Babs found Barrow knocking at the door of the ranch. It was Jeff who admitted him, regarding him suspiciously as, with an unusual quietness of manner, Barrow came into the living room.

'Losing your grip, Jeff?' the girl asked, glancing up from the table where she and Jeff had been glancing through a plan of the pipeline. 'What's the idea of letting this — double-crosser into the place? I can smell the air going rank bad already.'

'Thanks,' Poker said laconically.

'I let him in only because I'm interested in what he might have to say,' Jeff answered. 'I'm not particularly enjoying talking to you, Poker, after the way you framed me on that murder rap — '

'You were cleared, weren't you?' Barrow snapped. 'It was only a means to an end. I'd no intention of lettin' you swing for it — '

'Since I can't prove that I s'pose I'll have to think yore virtuous?' Jeff questioned. 'A nice, clean honest fighter who wouldn't dream of a stab in the back?'

'Meanin'?'

'Meanin' yore the sort who sends thousands of tons of rock down on my pipeline, kills three honest workers, and tries — no doubt of it — to kill me and Babs. Why, you reptile, I don't know why I don't blast the daylights out of you right where you stand!'

'Why blame that avalanche on me?' Barrow demanded, his voice injured. 'I didn't know anythin' about it until I discovered it had blocked my watercourse. You don't think I'd be fool enough to start an avalanche knowin' that it would do that to me, do you?'

'You probably didn't know it would,' Jeff retorted. 'Now it has you stymied — an' what in heck do you want here, anyway?'

Barrow hesitated, looking at the girl's set, uncompromising face, and then he said:

'I'm in a spot without water: I admit it. It's the life blood of a ranch, I reckon . . .'

'That doesn't interest me,' Babs said

coldly. 'After all you've done you've got your gall coming here and asking for help.'

'I'm not — but I'm willing to call off this pipeline war, give you all the help an' labour I can, an' pay five thousand dollars for the privilege of sharin' your pipeline. Half of it to turn your pastures, an' half to mine.'

The girl gave him one long look of contempt and turned back to studying the plan. Jeff looked from one to the other and then grinned cynically.

'There's your answer, Poker,' he said. 'Now get out.'

'But it doesn't make sense,' Barrow insisted. 'You can't use the water because it's blocked underground — at least you can't until you free it an' run it through a pipe. I can't use it either . . . So what's wrong with sharin'?'

'Everythin'!' Jeff told him. 'That stream is legally mine, don't forget, and to share it I'd have to have a document givin' you equal rights. From equal rights you'd mighty soon get a major hold somehow, knowin' all the dirty tricks you do — an' I'd find that pipeline all yours afore I could turn round. It'll stay all mine, or nothin'. Now get movin' . . . We're just not interested — an' if you try anythin' as we repair that pipeline yore liable to find yourself full of lead — or mebby yore ranch'll burn down — or somethin'. The gloves are off right now. That pipeline is going to be finished and you're going to be bushwhacked before I'm through with you. Now get!'

'I hope,' Barrow murmured, with a steely glance, 'neither of you is goin' to regret this . . . Somehow I have the feelin' that you are.'

He turned left, went down the porch steps to his horse, and mounted it. For a while he rode under the prairie stars, short-reining his horse presently so that he jog-trotted. Musing, he gazed into the distance where kerosene fires revealed that the pipeline men were still struggling to bring order out of chaos.

'I reckon there's still another ace in

the hole,' he muttered; and turning the horse's head he returned to within half a mile of the Double Circle ranch, tied the horse to a tree, and then went on foot for the remaining distance until he was near the Double Circle. Here he squatted down in the black shadow of a tree and gazed at the lights in the ranch-house.

In all, he remained in the vicinity of the tree for nearly two hours, only getting up and moving as the cold wind blew about him — then at last, a little while after midnight, he became more alert as the light from the living room window expired and another window lighted on the right of it. From frequent visits to the ranch he knew it to be the girl's bedroom. He waited until the lamplight was extinguished and the ranch was dark in the starlight. The vast wilderness was undisturbed, save for the distant pipeline night-shift.

Drawing out his gun he advanced silently, presently climbed the fence around the ranch-yard, and dropped to the other side of it. Without a sound he drifted from shadow to shadow, his gun cocked, until he came near to the girl's bedroom window. Here he paused. A figure was squatting, heavily dressed against the night bleakness, the barrel of a rifle glinting across his knee in the starshine.

Barrow grinned to himself and began a wide detour, finally coming up on the man from one side. Too late the sentry caught sight of him — Barrow dived, bringing down the butt of his .38 with all his force. The man crumpled motionless across his rifle. To Barrow it was only the work of a moment to drag the unconscious man into an outhouse and throw the rifle on top of him; then he crept forward again to the bedroom window.

Since it was slightly open at the top the bottom frame moved up easily enough. Disregarding caution any longer he pushed the sash up and wriggled himself to the ledge, pointing his .38 into the room beyond.

'Take it easy, Babs,' he murmured, as the girl, drowsy, was only just aware of what was happening. 'You an' me are goin' places. Get yourself dressed — an' be quick about it.'

'And if I don't?' she demanded angrily. 'What do you suppose you'd do?'

'Shoot you,' he answered. 'I don't say I'd kill you but I'd sure make you mighty uncomfortable — so stop arguin' and dress if you don't want to get hurt.'

Babs moved in the dim light and climbed out of bed. Barrow slid into the room, keeping near her in the gloom so that she had no opportunity to perhaps whisk a gun on him.

'Don't I even get a chance to dress in privacy?' she snapped.

'No. Put your overalls over that nightdress since yore so choosy — an' keep your voice down.'

In five minutes she had obeyed orders and he forced her out of the open window ahead of him, drawing the sash down silently after him. As she went across the yard with his gun jabbing in her back Babs deliberately scuffed the heels of her half-boots.

'Quiet!' Barrow breathed. 'In fact I'll make sure,' he added, and swept her up, struggling, into his arms, his powerful hands clamping over her mouth as she tried to scream.

He carried her over the fence and beyond the ranch, and so finally to his horse, where he lifted her up into the saddle. Then he untied the reins and leapt up behind her.

'If this doesn't bring that bone-headed friend of yours to his senses nothin' will,' he told her, spurring the animal. 'You'll see!'

8

Jeff Alroyd discovered Babs's disappearance early enough the following morning, and his first hope that she had perhaps gone out for exercise — or else had decided to go unusually early to help the pipeline men — was dashed when the still motionless labourer, who had been on sentry duty outside the girl's bedroom window, was found in the outhouse.

In the dawn light Jeff and a gathering of labourers from the bunkhouse looked down on the man.

'He's dead,' one of them announced, getting up. 'Skull's smashed. Whoever did it did it properly, I reckon.'

'Barrow!' Jeff breathed, clenching his fists. 'Couldn't ha' been anybody else. An' it's an even bet that he's also got Miss Babs . . . Okay, I'm goin' over to his place right now.'

'Want us?' one of the men demanded.

'No — I'll handle this myself. I may need you later, though.'

He turned away with swift, angry strides, saddled his mare, and rode it at break-neck speed down the valley until he came to the Lazy-Y. It almost seemed as though Barrow had been expecting his arrival for he was on the porch, apparently enjoying the morning air before the merciless blaze of the sun began to beat down.

'Well, if it isn't pretty boy Alroyd,' he commented cynically. 'Early call for you, isn't it?'

Tethering his mare to the porch rail Jeff hurried up the steps. He came straight to the point.

'Where's Babs?' he demanded.

Barrow lit a cigarette and blew the smoke in Jeff's face.

'Am I supposed to know?'

Savagely Jeff gripped the shoestring and dragged on it.

'So help me, Poker,' he breathed, 'if you've done anythin' to her I'll finish you — now!'

Barrow snatched himself away, but he made no attempt to draw his guns. Instead he stood looking at Jeff's levelled .45 as it sprang into his hand.

'Well?' Jeff demanded. 'What's the answer. You don't need to stall. I know you took Babs by force.'

'Clever of you,' Barrow murmured. 'An' take care how you use your gun. I've a ranch foreman and some twenty punchers just around the corner, don't forget. If you use that on me they'll blast you before you c'n even mount your horse.'

'It'd be worth it to drill you — Damn you, Poker, where's Babs?' Jeff roared at him.

'Safely tucked away.' Barrow gave a wide grin. 'An' you'll never find her — even less so if you drill me . . . I wouldn't have snatched her only it was th' only card I had left.' He drew pensively at his cigarette for a moment or two and then added, 'Y'see, Babs is liable to disappear from the face of the earth — nobody ever bein' able to prove what happened to her. I wouldn't mind blottin' her out because since you came on th' scene she's turned dead against me ... Only I don't like murder.'

'You don't eh?' Jeff smiled sourly. 'You didn't mind so much last night when you killed the guard outside her window.'

'Killed him, did I?' Barrow shook his head. 'That's just too bad. I didn't know I hit him that hard.'

'Later this mornin' I'm advisin' the sheriff about it,' Jeff said. 'And about you kidnappin' Babs, too. That's plumb against the law, Poker, and you know it.'

'Sure I know it — an' advise the sheriff all you want if it'll make you feel any better — but remember two things. You've no proof that I killed that sentry, an' if I get tied up with th' law neither you nor anybody else is goin' to see Babs Kemp ever again.'

Jeff kept his gun cocked. 'You didn't steal Babs just for th' heck of it, Barrow: you're not that loco, I reckon.

What's th' idea back of it?'

'Just this.' Barrow flipped his cigarette over the porch rail. 'That stream of yours is legally in your name: you got your claim in ahead of me. That pipeline is also yours since all th' bills are in your name. Now, if you'll sign the stream and pipeline over to me I'll hand Babs Kemp back to you within an hour — safe an' unhurt . . . If you don't you'll never see her again. An' searchin' for her won't do no good 'cos she's in a spot only I know about. Not even my outfit knows. That's why hogtying me with th' law would bring about her death.'

Jeff slowly returned his gun to its holster.

'I might ha' known you'd think of a trick like this,' he muttered. 'Usin' a girl to force your own ends . . . ' He sighed. 'Okay, you win. I can't gamble a stream an' a pipeline against the life of Babs. Come back to th' Double Circle with me an' I'll endorse the pipeline and stream deeds over to you.'

'I'm not comin' anywhere,' Barrow answered calmly. 'You might spring somethin' on me on your own territory an' I'm not that crazy. Bring the deed here, endorsed over to me, and I'll have lawyer Billings verify its validity this afternoon.'

'An' how do I know Babs will be freed?' Jeff asked grimly.

'I don't think you trust me,' Barrow remarked, grinning again. 'All I c'n do is have her within seein' distance when you bring that deed. If it's okay you can have the gal — unmolested. If it isn't — But I reckon it will be.' Barrow finished menacingly.

Jeff gave him a long, grim look and then made up his mind the only way it could be made up. He turned away.

'I'll be back in half an hour,' he said. 'See that you have Babs where I can spot her.'

Barrow nodded and Jeff vaulted into the saddle of his mare. He rode back swiftly to the Double Circle, to find the labourers waiting for him. They looked at him expectantly as he jumped down from his mount.

'I reckon Barrow's holdin' all the aces,' he told them bitterly, and briefly outlined the situation.

'But it's a plain give-away, Mr Alroyd!' one of them objected. 'Why can't we start a-searchin' for Miss Kemp?'

'Because th' risk to her is too great. Barrow isn't foolin': she'll die if we start crossin' him. Right now there's no other way out. I've got to sign everythin' over to him — far as the pipeline's concerned. As for you fellers, you might as well pack up and hit the trail for home. I'll have no further use for you that I can see.'

Set-faced, Jeff left them and strode into the ranch. It did not take him above five minutes to endorse the deed and sign it; then, with it in his pocket, he returned swiftly down the valley to find Barrow awaiting him at the gates of the Lazy-Y.

'There you are,' he said, and jerked his head.

Jeff glanced towards the corral. At the main entrance to it four of Barrow's men were standing, their guns ready. In their midst, powerless to do anything, Babs herself lounged against the nearest mesquite post. She gave Jeff one beseeching look.

'And here you are,' Jeff snapped, and handed over the deed.

Barrow took it, examined it carefully, and finally nodded.

'Yeah,' he acknowledged, 'I reckon that seems to cover everythin', assignin' all rights therein to me. Billings can check it but I know enough about legal documents to see that this one is okay. Right! I'll have my men get busy freein' that stream and divertin' the pipe — '

'And what about Babs?' Jeff demanded.

'Impatient ain't you?' Barrow grinned; then he signalled. 'Okay, boys — let her go!'

Immediately Babs began running across the enclosure, only pausing when she had reached Jeff. He put a protecting arm about her shoulders.

'Good as my word, y'see,' Barrow remarked dryly. 'All right — get off my land th' pair of you!'

Jeff set his mouth and lifted the girl up into the saddle. He swung up behind her and set the mare jogging slowly along the valley.

'What did he do to you?' he presently asked the girl.

'Shut me in one of the old goldmine excavations about two miles away. I thought I was due to stop there forever until he released me not so long ago . . . ' The girl's voice was low and dispirited.

'You don't have to tell me what happened, Jeff: he took good care to give me all the facts . . . The pipeline and stream against my life.'

'I had to give in,' Jeff told her quietly. 'No choice. But mebby we'll think of somethin'.'

'Maybe — but I doubt it. Far as I can see there are no tricks left, on either side. Poker played his last one, and it turned up trumps.'

In a setting of complete despondency they finished the ride up the valley to find the pipeline men busy with their preparations for departure. A buckboard was loaded with their belongings. The foreman-labourer stood waiting as the two came up.

'I aim to drive th' boys to the station with their stuff, boss,' he said, 'then I'll bring th' buckboard back. After that I'll be on my way, too.'

'Okay,' Jeff sighed. 'Best of luck, fellers. Sorry it had to work out this way.'

'I still think that low down chiseller Barrow needs some slugs in th' belly,' the foreman muttered.

'Maybe he does,' Babs said, as Jeff lifted her from the saddle, 'but it wouldn't get us anywhere — 'cept maybe under a gallows. Best forget it . . . '

She preceded Jeff into the ranch house and he flung down his hat savagely.

'If only I could think of somethin'!' he exclaimed. 'But with no money, no pipeline, and no water — What's the use?'

186

The girl did not answer. She was too lost in sombre speculations. Finally she went into the kitchen and got a meal and some coffee together. She and Jeff were half way through the meal when a sudden dull concussion made them glance at each other. They both rose and went out on to the porch.

'Blastin',' Jeff commented, nodding to a mushroom of smoke drifting from the mountain side in the hot, brilliant air. 'He doesn't waste much time, does he? He's trying already to free that blocked stream.'

Babs was silent, her eyes on the distant band of workers whom Barrow had evidently brought from his ranch to begin operations. There were two more concussions and drifting smoke. The girl went slowly back to the table and Jeff followed her, seating himself and picking up his coffee cup.

'I suppose,' Babs said, musing, 'when you are beaten it is only commonsense to admit the fact?'

'Depends if we are — '

'Oh why try and blind yourself, Jeff?' she cried. 'We are, and there's no disguising it. The only thing we can do is get out. We can't live on a dead ranch with no hope of ever getting water for the pastures.'

He drank in silence for a while and then sighed.

'Yeah, I suppose yore right, Babs . . . What do you suggest then?'

'Selling — to Poker. The spread, the land, everything. Then we can get out.' The girl smiled faintly. 'Or is it an assumption my saying 'we'?'

'It's th' only bright spot in a gloomy picture,' Jeff answered her. 'An' I reckon it's the only sensible way out. We could go to Kansas an' I'd settle down at some minin' engineering again — leastways until I got footloose again . . . It's a dog-gone shame, though. I'd great hopes of buildin' somethin' worthwhile outa this land around here.'

'Without Barrow we could've . . . ' The girl thought out the problem for a long time, then she turned and went out on to the porch again. Jeff got up and joined her.

'Poker's with his men over there,' she said. 'I can see him. I'll go over and tell him that we — '

'You mean I will,' Jeff interrupted. 'I wouldn't trust that polecat near you for two seconds. Get out the deeds of property whilst I go and tip him off.'

She nodded and Jeff went down the porch steps to his mare. He was back again in fifteen minutes, Barrow riding beside him. The big rancher was grinning cynically as he came into the living room.

'Must be my lucky day, Babs,' he commented, as the girl sat at the table. 'The pipeline, the ranch, and the land all at once. Only bad streak is that I don't get you too . . . You an' me, with all th' money I've got, could've gone a long ways together.'

'I happen to be one piece of 'property' you can't buy,' Babs answered him coldly.

'Up to you. You shouldn't let your

heart run away with your head . . . '
Barrow threw off his hat and sat down
at the table. 'Well, what gives? Alroyd
here says you want to sell your spread
an' then vamoose.'

'That's right. How much will you
give for it?'

'Well now . . . ' Barrow cocked a
critical eye about him. 'I should think
about . . . a thousand dollars.'

'One miserable thousand!' the girl
ejaculated, astounded. 'But that's only
half of what it was before! The cattle are
still capable of being restored to health.
With water you can — '

'Thousand's the best I can do,'
Barrow snapped. 'Stop tryin' to be
fancy, Babs. You c'n have a thousand
for it, an' clear out — takin' Alroyd
with you; or you c'n have nothin' and
be forced to go anyway because you've
no water. Take your choice. I've no time
to play around.'

A distant explosion made him glance
up. 'That's why,' he added. 'I ought to
be supervising that blastin'. Water's

liable to be freed any minute.'

The girl gave Jeff a glance and he nodded.

'All right,' she assented bitterly. 'Nothing much else I can do, I suppose — But I want cash on the nail.'

Barrow got to his feet. 'You can have it. I'll ride back to my spread and get the money for you. While I'm gone get those deeds signed over t'me. This afternoon I'll have Billings give them the once over.'

He turned and strode out of the room. The girl unscrewed the top of the ink bottle and looked moodily at the land agreement.

'There's no other way, Babs,' Jeff said quietly, patting her shoulder. 'We'll make up for it one day. Better sign.'

She nodded and dipped the pen in the ink — then she paused with it held over the deed. It was shivering mysteriously, so was the table; so was the floor. It grew to a positive vibration . . .

'What's — what's happening?' she asked blankly, as a growling, muttering, roar became slowly apparent.

She jumped up, the deed forgotten, and with Jeff dashed to the porch. Neither of them needed to speak: their eyes were taking in the incredible scene across the valley.

Apparently water had been released — with a vengeance! From half way up the mountain range a gigantic flood was rolling, sweeping rocks before it, obliterating the men working on the pipeline, tumbling in an ever-growing, deluging thunder towards the valley.

Some little distance away, Barrow, astride his horse, had also seen the approaching cataclysm. He suddenly put on speed literally racing for his life.

'It's a flood!' the girl shouted, horrified. 'Jeff! That's no stream! It's a huge underground river or something — And we're right in its track!'

Jeff snapped abruptly into action and caught her arm.

'Out — quick!' he ordered. 'It's our only chance.'

He hurtled her down the porch steps

and pushed her up into the mare's saddle. Springing up beside her he turned the mare's head and began a desperate ride away from the ranch by the back route, speeding as fast as he could possibly go — but even so he was nowhere near fast enough to escape that vast, tumbling deluge raging down into the valley.

One glance back assured Jeff and the girl that the fifty-foot wall of wave surging towards them was infinitely swifter than the mare they rode. The Double Circle ranch smashed into ruins beneath the flood. The cattle were borne up in it. Uprooted trees collapsed and vanished in the boiling smother.

In the far distance Barrow was overwhelmed and disappeared from sight — Then Jeff and the girl abruptly found themselves struggling deep in a frothing wilderness of water, torn from the mare, striking upwards as they fought frantically for air.

Jeff bobbed to the surface first to find himself being swept along in the torrent. It had reached its highest level now in the valley and was rolling northwards in a steady flow, following the natural course of the former arid valley floor. Of the Double Circle or Lazy-Y, there was no longer any sign. Only surging waters, struggling cattle and horses, uprooted trees and fence posts —

'Babs!' Jeff shouted frantically. 'Babs, where are you?'

For several moments he could see no sign of her; then he caught a glimpse of a shoulder and head bobbing momentarily over the flood a quarter of a mile from him. He struck out towards the figure and came upon the girl. A streak of blood across her forehead showed where she had been struck by a tree branch or some such obstacle.

Jeff supported her chin with one arm and struck out with the other, dragging her along beside him. He was forced to follow the current for nearly two miles, and in the process he passed the splintered remains of the Lazy-Y, past which the river was now racing. He had one glimpse of a body impaled on the savagely sharp projection branch of a tree —

Fighting and struggling, and diagonal to the current, he came at last to shelving ground and staggered up it. Carefully he dragged the girl out beside him and laid her down amidst the rocks. Their saturated clothes began to steam heavily in the blaze of the sun.

To Jeff's intense relief the blow on the girl's head was only superficial. He wiped away the blood streaks and fastened a wet handkerchief round the gash; then at last he was rewarded by seeing the girl open her eyes.

'What-what happened?' she whispered, wincing and then staring at him. 'Jeff — you all right — ? Gosh, my head! What hit it?'

He put his arm behind her shoulders and raised her so that she could gaze out over the waste of water.

'Our river — in our valley,' he murmured. Then he said: 'It was probably a tree branch which hit you — Look at all the water, Babs! A ranch perched on the edge of this will be the most thrivin' in the district!'

'If Poker lets it,' she responded gloomily.

'He'll never bother us, or anybody else, again,' Jeff told her quietly. 'I passed him when I was dragging you down river. He'd gotten a tree branch right through his belly — instead of bullets — but the effect's the same, I reckon. We've won, Babs. His men are gone too. Looks as if we're th' only survivors.'

'But what happened?' she asked in wonder. 'Where on earth did this river come from?'

'I can only think of one answer — as a minin' engineer. This river must always have been underground, dammed back by rock. As long as a stream flowed it worked as a safety valve an' the pressure was kept even. But when it got blocked the water must ha' been buildin' up to a terrific pressure behind the rocks. We

196

call that 'osmosis' in mining terms. Then, when those men started blastin', the rocks fractured an' the pent-up deluge just blew itself forth . . . an' here it is! A baby Colorado if ever there was one!'

'And we can start again — and succeed,' Babs said slowly, her eyes brightening. 'That is — when we've got some money from somewheres.'

'I can play poker,' Jeff grinned, hugging her. 'An' from what I c'n remember my wife-to-be isn't so bad at it either!'

THE END

We do hope that you have enjoyed reading this large print book.

Did you know that all of our titles are available for purchase?

We publish a wide range of high quality large print books including:
**Romances, Mysteries, Classics
General Fiction
Non Fiction and Westerns**

Special interest titles available in large print are:
**The Little Oxford Dictionary
Music Book, Song Book
Hymn Book, Service Book**

Also available from us courtesy of Oxford University Press:
**Young Readers' Dictionary
(large print edition)
Young Readers' Thesaurus
(large print edition)**

For further information or a free brochure, please contact us at:
**Ulverscroft Large Print Books Ltd.,
The Green, Bradgate Road, Anstey,
Leicester, LE7 7FU, England.
Tel:** (00 44) **0116 236 4325**
Fax: (00 44) **0116 234 0205**